THE BONUS INK SET

A MONTGOMERY INK WORLD ANTHOLOGY

CARRIE ANN RYAN

The Bonus Ink Box Set
A Montgomery Ink World Anthology
By: Carrie Ann Ryan
© 2019 Carrie Ann Ryan
ISBN: 978-1-947007-96-3

Cover Art by Charity Hendry

For more information, please join Carrie Ann Ryan's MAILING LIST. To interact with Carrie Ann Ryan, you can join her FAN CLUB

THE BONUS BOX INK SET

NYT Bestselling author Carrie Ann Ryan brings you three Montgomery Ink world romances that will tug at your heart and make your pulse bound. And because sometimes the romance isn't over at the end of the book, The Bonus Ink Box set includes seven additional short stories and deleted scenes from the Montgomery Ink World!

Executive Ink (A Montgomery Ink Romance)

Ashylnn didn't want him...she craved him. That was her first mistake, but not her last. She's the boss of her life and decisions. She doesn't have time for a bearded, inked man. But he may just make her yearn for it.

Jax thought it would only be for one night but now he

wants more. She's the straight-laced executive to his leather-and-jeans life, and she makes him desire more. She is so much more. But how much, he may never know.

Second Chance Ink (A Montgomery Ink Romance)

Tattoo artist Brandon never thought he'd see her again. He'd trained himself never to think of her or what they'd had together. It was the only way he'd been able to survive but now she's standing right in front of him and he can hardly breathe.

Lauren hadn't known he'd be part of her plans until it was too late. She'd thought he was gone from her life and memories forever. Now he's in her orbit once more and she'll have to fight to remember the girl she once was and the woman she's become.

Ink by Numbers (A Montgomery Ink: Colorado Springs Romance)

Kaylee knows art, friendship, and love. And because she's known love, she wants nothing to do with it ever again. She likes her life just the way it is. Her art and her Brushes with Lushes classes keep her sane and happy.

Landon spends his days with numbers and financial spreadsheets. At night, he just wants to relax, but the only way he can do that is with a woman. But these days, not just any woman will do.

Kaylee and Landon do an excellent job of dancing around each other, but no matter how much desire burns between them or their own personal hang-ups, they'll need to make a choice: life as they know it, or a life that could be so much more.

EXECUTIVE INK

A MONTGOMERY INK ROMANCE

Ashylnn didn't want him...she *craved* him. That was her first mistake, but not her last. She's the boss of her life and decisions. She doesn't have time for a bearded, inked man. But he may just make her yearn for it.

Jax thought it would only be for one night but now he wants more. She's the straight-laced executive to his leather-and-jeans life, and she makes him desire more. She *is* so much more. But how much, he may never know.

Author Note: Executive Ink is a Montgomery Ink short story and a little different than what you're used to from me. It's shorter than my other novellas at only ~12,000 words. It has a complete HEA, and is perfect for a steamy evening, one-sitting read.

CHAPTER 1

*E*xhaustion crept over Ashlynn Kelly's body, but she ignored it, pushing it deep down where she knew it would stay until she found time to actually take care of it. Much like she ignored the fact that her feet had gone numb about two hours ago in her red-soled stilettos, and how her back ached enough that she knew it would take at least three hour-long massages to get out the kinks. Of course, by the time she arranged appointments with her massage therapist, she'd need even more hours with him, and she'd be down another pair of shoes.

But she'd closed the damn deal.

Nothing could take that away from her.

Not even blisters on her feet and a throbbing temple or two or even the muggy Atlanta air.

She'd spent her life working countless hours and

barely sleeping while dealing with condescending men in business suits. Guys who traveled on Mondays to get to out-of-town business meetings while laughing far too loudly and looking at her legs rather than her face before flying back home Friday evenings with even more leers. She'd dealt with them during *her* meetings as they called her "honey," and flashed them her patented icy glare when they gave her their coffee orders before every conference or panel instead of treating her like an equal. She'd gotten her MBA while working two jobs and dealt with men who only looked at her for her tits and pins— their words, not hers—not her brain.

Now, she was the CFO of a *Forbes* 500 company and kicking genuine ass.

At least, this week.

So, yes, her feet hurt, and she had a headache from hell, but there were no mediocre men with fat egos around to piss her off. Only, she had a feeling as soon as she walked back into the hotel lobby, she'd be surrounded by those blowhards in suits and loosened ties. She'd been in the conference center across the street most of the day, and rather than walk the extra mile to use the covered bridge that connected the two buildings, she'd opted to go outside and breathe some fresh air for what felt like the first time in weeks.

Between meetings, panels, lunches on the premises, and dinners that had, for some reason, only occurred in the revolving restaurant on-site, she'd spent her entire week breathing hotel and conference room air.

As soon as her crosswalk light turned green, Ashlynn inhaled a deep breath and almost choked. It was a little too humid and damp at the moment for that kind of breathing, and she knew the underneath layers of her hair were starting to curl. *That* was why she'd spent the days inside rather than out. Her throat might be dry and her skin in need of some serious lotion time thanks to the acrid air of the hotel, but her hair and makeup had stayed in place for the ten hours she'd needed it to throughout the day.

At the moment, however, she didn't give a damn how she looked. She'd made the deal, gotten her company's name in the hands of the few people at the event who didn't know about them and had even impressed the good ol' boys who thought her a stripper rather than their potential rival.

Silly men and their tiny dicks in this business, she thought. They never saw her coming until it was far too late and she'd walked all over them, wrapping them around her finger at the same time for good measure.

Ashlynn was damn good at what she did, and when she got home, she'd open a bottle of wine to celebrate.

By herself.

Because it wasn't as if she had time these days to actually go out and meet someone, let alone get to know them enough to bring them into her life like that. She hadn't had sex with another person in months, but that was fine. She had her hand, and a nice selection of vibrators—one that even blew little puffs of air right on her clit and made her come in five seconds flat—she didn't need a man.

Though a hot night of sex with no commitments might be nice one day. Just meaningless, against-the-door sex with a man who loved going down on her until she came over and over again before fucking her hard into the mattress until he released himself all over her. Just downright dirty, unhinged, no holds barred sex.

Ashlynn swallowed hard. *Yes*, that *would be nice.*

Not that she'd actually get that in her hotel at the moment since she knew probably half the men down in the bar area. That meant she needed to remain her professional, icy self and make use of the showerhead in her hotel bathroom when she got back up to her room. There was no way she'd sleep with someone in her profession—not when that would rebound on her. God forbid a woman want a night of hot sex without being labeled a slut. The rest of her coworkers could get away with that because they were men, but not her. She had to remain aboveboard because double standards were still a thing, no matter how many marches she attended or how hard she tapped that glass ceiling—at least for now, damn it.

It wasn't as if she were the only woman in this position either. Her company had more women than it had before—thanks to her—but she was the only one at this particular conference since it was her project on the line. Ashlynn didn't know the other women attending this week that well since they hadn't been in her panels as they each had their own jobs to do, so she was pretty much on her own. And while that suited her most days, tonight, she was a bit lonely.

Ashlynn shook her head as she stepped onto the pavement that separated the two large streets she'd had to cross in order to get back to her hotel. The pedestrian crossing lights were so short that it took two cycles to get from one side to the other—even with her power walk in heels.

Tapping her foot, she looked around at the traffic surrounding her and tried not to sway from foot to foot. Her feet *hurt*. Maybe she didn't need hot sex; a foot massage might be enough. Sadly, she knew from experience that doing it herself just wasn't quite the same— much like an orgasm, but that was something she wasn't going to think about.

The red hand went away, and the little man lit up, so she looked both ways—as people were idiots when it came to driving no matter what state you were in—and stepped into the crosswalk. She'd almost made it to the other side when bright lights came at her, and she did the one thing she'd sworn never to do in an intense situation —something she'd never done before.

She froze.

Strong hands wrapped around her middle and tugged her to the side of the road, and her toe caught on the curb. With an *oof*, she found herself lying on a hard, male chest, a large hand on her waist, the other on her head as if protecting her, even though she'd been the one to land on him.

"You okay, princess?" the man rumbled. Yes, rumbled —she could feel the sound of his growl of a voice under her hands. She blinked down at him, the adrenaline pounding in her system and making it hard for her to catch her breath. The man beneath her wore a T-shirt with some logo on the front, and from what she could feel beneath her legs, he also wore jeans. His hair was a tad too long, and his beard was scruffy yet oddly sexy. And the ink she caught a glimpse of? *Oh, my.*

Maybe she'd hit her head when she fell.

"Princess?"

"Don't call me princess." Not the thank you she'd planned on saying, but clearly, she wasn't thinking straight.

He smirked at her, but it wasn't like the ones the men in suits usually gave her. Instead, this one heated her inner thighs, and she really hated him for it.

"If you can snap at me like that, you should be okay.

Want me to let you up, or would you rather lay sprawled like this outside? I don't mind it much since having a sexy woman on top of me is never a hardship, but I'm pretty sure there's a rock underneath my back digging into my spine that'll probably hurt in the morning."

Ashlynn scrambled off him, aware that she *never* scrambled. She was far too put-together for that, but she supposed nearly being run over by a car would do that to any woman. The man put a hand on her hip as she stood with him, and she took a step to the side, needing her space. He might have saved her life, but she didn't know this man, and for some reason, he screamed *danger* to her instincts. Not his looks since menace could wear suits just as well as ink, but she could still sense something that told her to walk away and never look back.

"Thank you for getting me out of the way," she said stiffly. "I shouldn't have frozen like that." She was *so* pissed at herself for not reacting quickly enough.

The man in front of her frowned. "No need to thank me, princess. And you didn't freeze. Not really. Everything happened so quickly that I'm pretty sure you could have saved yourself. I just helped it along since that asshole didn't even stop after running that red." He shrugged and stuffed his hands into his pockets. "Anyway, I'd still be sure to check for any bruises." He blinked when she narrowed her eyes at him. "Not meaning me, though I wouldn't say no since you're damn sexy right now with that glare of yours. I meant you, or your doctor or something. You want me to walk you to your hotel just to be sure?"

She shook her head. "I'm fine, but thank you again."

"No problem. Just keep a lookout for rogue cars." He nodded and started back to the hotel behind them. *Her hotel.*

That was a little too coincidental for her to keep up the icy act she'd perfected. "Are you staying here?" she asked his back.

He turned and raised a sexy brow. Who knew brows could be sexy? "Yeah. You?"

She nodded and licked her lips. It had to be the adrenaline making her want to say what she was about to say. But a girl didn't land on a sexy as hell man in the middle of a sidewalk every day.

"Can I buy you a drink?" Her nipples tightened. Adrenaline. Had to be the adrenaline. "To say thank you."

His gaze met hers before he smiled widely—not that smirk he'd given her before, but a bright grin surrounded by a big beard. A smile that once again went straight to the center of her thighs and made her knees weak.

"I'm Jax, princess, and I think a drink sounds perfect."

"Ashlynn. I'm Ashlynn." *And I'm about to do the most reckless thing I've ever done in my life.*

· · ·

JAX PRESSED HER BACK AGAINST THE HOTEL DOOR, AND SHE moaned into his mouth, not able to get enough of him. He tasted of the beer he'd had when she bought him that drink in the hotel bar, though she couldn't remember what she'd ordered. She'd ignored the blatant stares from those she knew in the bar and would ignore them from here on out if they gave her any shit.

The man currently licking her ear and biting down on the lobe wasn't any of those men. He was *hers*. Just for this night—and that's exactly how she wanted it.

His beard wasn't as scruffy as she thought it would be. Instead, it was soft and slid against her skin in a delicious way that had her thinking about what it would feel like when he ate her out.

Not *if. When.*

Because she'd damn well get that talented tongue of his between her thighs tonight. That was a given.

"Damn, princess, you can kiss," Jax breathed as he licked up her neck.

Seriously, the man had a talented tongue.

"Call me Ashlynn," she panted, sliding her hands under his shirt so she could feel the heat of his skin beneath her fingertips. "I'm no princess."

He moved to cup her face and kiss her hard, his tongue sliding across hers in an erotic caress. "But you look like a dark-haired version of that icy one from the movie with that song that I'm not going to sing or we'll end up having it stuck in our heads for the next six months."

And now she would be singing it for at least that long. *Thank you, Jax.*

She raised a brow even as her eyes rolled to the back of her head when he sucked on the place where her shoulder met her neck. "She was a *queen,* and animated. I don't look like her."

He kissed her hard again on the lips. "You have her eyes. And that attitude."

"Call me Ashlynn if you want to finish what we started here. Because I won't just be a random woman for the evening. Tomorrow, when we part ways and never see each other again, you can think of me as princess all you want. Tonight? Tonight, I'm Ashlynn. Got me?"

Jax grinned this time, and it was a new smile to her. He had so many expressions, and she'd only just met the man. "I can do that, *Ashlynn.* As long as I get to suck on these tits of yours that have been talking to me since they were pressed against my chest, and as long as I can taste that pussy of yours that has pretty much drenched my thigh since you straddled me. Does that sound like a plan?"

She swallowed hard, her clit throbbing in response to his words. No need to be embarrassed when she could see his arousal just as well as he could feel hers. "As long as you fuck me, too. Because I'm going to need this cock of yours inside me." She reached between them and gripped the long line of him through his jeans. "Does *that* sound like a plan?"

He growled low in his throat, and she barely kept from pressing her legs together to relieve the ache. "We're wearing too many clothes for this." Then he gripped the back of her hair and tugged, pulling her head back so he could devour her mouth with his.

They pulled on each other's clothes, practically tearing them from their bodies. There was no finesse here, no tease of temptation. This was all need pounding through them as they learned one another.

Ashlynn reached between them, wrapping her fingers around his hard length. Of course, since this had to all be a dream, her fingers couldn't quite touch each other around the base.

Best. Fantasy. Ever.

"Jesus, Ash," Jax growled out. "You're gonna make me blow my load before I even get to taste your cunt. And believe me, I need to get a taste of you." He squeezed his hand over hers with a groan before pulling away. "On your back, Ash. I need you."

"Ashlynn. I'm Ashlynn." She never shortened her name, never wanted to be a pile of burned embers, the remnants of the woman she'd once been.

He kissed her again, and she almost forgot her name entirely. "You're my Ash. My Ashlynn. Just for tonight, remember." He winked at her. "I promise to respect you in the morning."

She laughed at the joke before letting out a little gasp when he tossed her onto the bed behind them. Before she could scold him for throwing her around like a sack of potatoes, she screamed his name as he buried his face between her thighs.

"Jesus," she panted when he lapped at her clit, his beard scraping her skin in such a way that it nearly sent her over the edge of bliss. He sucked and licked until she arched against him, coming so hard that she didn't have the air in her lungs to even call out his name.

Her nipples ached, and her breasts were heavy, so she lazily pinched the nubs between her fingers, still needing relief even while Jax licked up her orgasm.

"Those are mine for the night, Ash."

She blinked up at him in a haze as he leaned down and sucked a nipple into his mouth. "Damn," she breathed.

He chuckled against her, his beard scraping her overly sensitive skin. "You taste fucking sweet. I'm going to enjoy fucking that tight pussy of yours tonight. You still okay with this?" He kissed her breasts then met her eyes. "Because we can stop if you want to. Just say the word, and I'll walk out of here without another word if this is too much for you."

For some reason, the care in his words made her

choke up, and she hated herself for that. This was just meaningless sex, and it would do her well to remember that.

"Thanks for your concern, but I see a *very* thick and hard cock in front of me that needs to be inside me. So, if you aren't going to get the job done, then I'll just use my fingers on myself and leave you hurting. How does that sound?" Knowing she sounded like a bitch, she added, "Plus, I need to repay the favor, Jax. I want you. Right now. Just you and me for one night, remember?"

He leaned down and kissed her so softly it was just a bare brush of lips. "I remember. Just checking, Ashlynn. Don't want to hurt you."

"You can't hurt me." A lie. It was always a lie, but one she'd perfected.

He met her gaze. "Okay, then. Let me wrap up because I want you safe." He shuffled to his jeans and pulled out his wallet and a condom before meeting her gaze as he rolled the latex down his length. "Ready for me?"

In answer, she cupped her breast and slid her other hand between her legs. "Hurry."

He was on her in a flash, sliding into her in one deep thrust. They both let out a gasp, but he didn't pause. Instead, he pounded into her, edging her closer and closer until all she could feel was him inside and the heat of her need. Then she came with a groan, her inner walls clamping around him, hard.

Jax kissed her fiercely again as he came, his hips moving at such a vigorous pace that she had a feeling they'd both be sore in the morning. She clung to him, her orgasm slowly fading but her need for him anything but.

Yet this was only one night. And when she left in the morning, she'd never look back. She couldn't afford to.

There would be no last names. No numbers exchanged. No promises.

This was all she needed.

At least that's what she told herself.

CHAPTER 2

*J*ax Reagan shouldn't have been surprised when he'd woken up the previous morning to an empty bed, but damned if he wasn't disappointed. He'd had the best sex of his life, and Ashlynn had left him when he slept without a backwards glance. Yeah, what they'd done was spontaneous, and they'd made no promises, but he still thought he'd have been the one to leave.

He'd never had a woman leave *him* sleeping in bed before, and while he wasn't sure how he felt about that, he knew there was nothing he could do. He didn't live in Atlanta anymore and wasn't going back anytime soon. He'd only been there to finish up a final job for a previous client he hadn't wanted to deal with in the first place. But his old boss still held a few strings Jax hadn't been able to sever until last night. So, Jax had flown from his new home in Denver to Atlanta to finish a tattoo he'd started the year before and hadn't wanted to fly back that night. Instead, he'd used his buddy's points and stayed at a hotel he normally wouldn't have paid for, but his friend had insisted. Jax had figured he'd spend the night watching a movie and sinking into decent sheets.

Instead, he'd sunk into something way more than decent.

Ashlynn. Ash. Princess.

The executive to his ink.

And he'd never see her again.

And what a damn shame that was—and not just because they'd fucked until the wee hours of the morning and he still hadn't gotten enough. No, he *liked* her. He'd only gotten to know her a little bit, but he liked what he saw. And he had to be honest that pulling her out of harm's way the first time he saw her had sent him over the edge just a little bit.

But now he'd have to put her out of his mind because he was back in Denver and working a half shift for the day at his new place of business. Montgomery Ink was a fantastic and popular tattoo shop in the heart of downtown Denver. A brother and sister who seemed to have around forty other family members coming and going from the black and hot pink doors at all hours of the day ran the place.

Austin and Maya treated him right, gave him the hours he needed, and actually cared about the ink they were hired to create.

That meant it was only about a thousand times better than his previous job.

Jax held back a shudder as he opened his sketchbook to work on his next project. Hell, his last place had been a dump where he'd been the best artist there, though that wasn't saying much. He'd made practically no money since his boss, Sammy, took a large cut for himself for one reason or another. Jax figured Sammy was in so deep with the mob and in so much debt that he needed Jax's ink money day in and day out.

And now that Jax wasn't there, Sammy wasn't making the kind of money he used to, and Jax had to deal with the endless texts and phone calls from his old boss.

Sammy wanted him back, and what Sammy wanted, Sammy got.

Only Jax didn't want to go back. He liked Montgomery Ink and enjoyed being out from under the mob's thumb. Luckily, he'd never dealt with them personally, but he'd been close enough to know fear when he scented it on the air.

In fact, he'd had a run-in with Sammy and a few men that Jax didn't really want to identify before he ran in to Ashlynn—literally—on the sidewalk. The guys had found him a few blocks down, and Jax had just escaped with a few short words when he saw the car coming at Ash down the street. It had scared him shitless to see her in harm's way, and he had reacted without thinking by pulling her toward him. It was something he hoped anyone would have done, but he wasn't so sure these days. Not with the hell he'd been through recently.

He blew out a breath and ran his hands over his beard. But now he was home, and hopefully done with Sammy's Ink and his crew. The only thing he regretted about any of that was that he'd never see Ashlynn again. He didn't know where she lived, but he had a feeling it wasn't in Atlanta since it looked as if she was in the hotel for a conference.

Jax guessed one night of hot sex and unforgettable tastes and touches would have to do him for a while.

It was a damn shame.

"You good over there, or do you need a minute to yourself?" Austin Montgomery teased from over in his booth. The Montgomery Ink set-up was similar to the other shops Jax had worked in. There were booths lined up on two sides of the large room, and each artist had his own workspace that he or she could make their own depending on what they needed. A couple of new rooms had been added recently—the privacy room with curtains they used for those who needed it, and a piercing room. There were also three booths in the back for rotating and visiting artists; Jax had one of those spots now. He was still new enough that he worked full-time hours but wasn't a full member of Montgomery Ink yet. He'd have to work up to that like everyone else who worked for the Montgomerys, and if he were lucky, he'd stay for longer than a month or two like some of the people that came and went.

"Jax?" Derek asked from the booth next to him. "You good? You didn't even rise to the bait with Austin's joke."

Jax shook his head and gave Austin a look. "Oh, I heard it. I was just 'taking a minute to myself.'"

His boss rolled his eyes and grinned. "Just don't jerk off in your booth. That'd be hell to clean up. For you. Because there are things friends and co-workers don't need to see or think about. And especially not do."

Jax flipped him off before turning to a blank page in his sketchbook. He had a client coming in who wanted a small dragon on his ribs. The client had been adamant about the size and placement, and Jax hadn't been able to dissuade him. The problem with the level of detail a dragon required was that it looked like crap on a smaller scale—and the ribcage was the *worst* for things like that. So, Jax would have to figure out a compromise because there was no way he'd give this guy a crappy tattoo.

Finding the balance between a client's needs and what could actually be done was the main part of his job. At least, it was *supposed* to be a big component. It hadn't always been like that when he worked for Sammy, and he'd hated it. He'd been bogged down by the drama of the shop and everything that came with that. It wasn't until he finally got his mom and sister out of the city and into Denver that he'd been able to get out from under Sammy's thumb.

Someone nudged his shoulder, and Jax looked up to see Austin frowning at him. "What?" he asked, his voice hoarse. He hadn't slept that well the night before since he was thinking of his time with Ashlynn and he was starting to feel it.

"You look like shit, man," Austin said with a frown. "Go catch a power nap on the couch Maya keeps in the office. It's still early enough that you won't have a walk-in, and you're clear on the books until this afternoon anyway since you planned to take your sister out to lunch."

Jax shook his head, feeling like an idiot for disappointing his new boss. He liked the Montgomerys and didn't want to screw things up because he wasn't sleeping. "I'm good."

Austin sighed. "No, you aren't. Just take a nap. We've all been there. Either that or chug some coffee. Hailey next door knows your order by now, and since that woman seems to have a sixth sense with these things, she's probably already making it."

Sloane, the other tattoo artist in the room, grinned. "My woman knows what she's doing." Hailey and Sloane were married, though Jax didn't know the details of how the sweet woman who owned the café next door had gotten together with the big and brash, inked man who worked with Jax, but he figured it was a good story.

"She does make damn fantastic brownies," Jax said, his stomach rumbling. "Think she'd let me have one for breakfast?" He was already up, feeling a little peppier at the thought.

Sloane snorted. "For you? Sure. For me? Not so much. Apparently, at my 'old age' I need to start thinking about my sugar intake."

Austin flipped them both off. "I'm older than both of you, so screw you. But, really, if you don't want the nap, go get some caffeine and maybe get us some, too." He winked. "Hailey will know our orders."

Jax laughed and made his way to the door that connected the two shops. "You really just wanted me to get up and get your coffees."

Austin gave him a mock salute that didn't look out of place with his big beard—the thing rivaled Jax's for sure. "Now you're getting it, young one."

"I'm not that much younger than you," Jax put in. He was in his thirties, just like Austin, and had lived through hell. Then again, he figured the Montgomerys had probably gone through some stuff of their own.

"True, but you're still the newbie in the shop," Austin joked, and Jax flipped the crew off before heading into the café. He couldn't help but smile as he did so, feeling more at home at Montgomery Ink in the few short weeks he'd worked there than the years he'd worked at Sammy's.

A change of scenery was good for me, he thought, just like the move had been needed for the rest of his family.

Now, he just had to make sure he didn't screw it all up.

JAX LOOKED DOWN AT HIS UN-TUCKED, BLACK, BUTTON-down shirt over jeans and winced. He probably should have changed into slacks or something to pick up his sister Jessica from her job so they could grab lunch. She was on her second week of being a paid intern at a major company, and was just now letting him pick her up for lunch. She didn't have much time off and was working crazier hours than he was, but he was so damned proud of her.

She was over ten years his junior and his perfect baby sister. She'd worked her butt off during college and had graduated with not only honors but also a position at a prestigious company in downtown Denver. Considering the state of the economy and the debt people her age were in these days, he knew she was not only talented but also lucky.

How his tattoo artist self had ended up with a corporate ladder-climbing baby sister, he didn't know, but he figured it hadn't been all him helping her get where she was. Their mother had worked her tail off at two jobs to keep a roof over their heads when he was a kid, so raising Jessica had been a group effort.

At least, that's what his mother said. If you asked him, Jessica had done pretty well on her own with his hovering and glares at anyone who dared come near her. She'd been the first in his family to finish college, and one of the few to even attempt it. *No one* was going to ruin this for her. Not even him.

But maybe he should have worn something other than jeans. At least there weren't any holes in them, and he was wearing a shirt that covered most of his ink. He'd thought about rolling down his sleeves to cover the tattoos on his forearms, but he figured that would be pushing it.

He looked up at the high-rise building that was one of the many that dotted the Denver skyline and couldn't help but grin. He'd always thought the tall buildings looked so tiny compared to the dramatic backdrop of the Rockies behind them, but standing next to one and knowing Jessica worked inside just made him realize how far she'd come. He couldn't wait to see where she went next.

Still grinning, he walked into the building and ignored the curious looks from people in stuffy suits and ties. He couldn't help but think of Ashlynn at that moment and how out of place he'd looked next to her, but damn if they hadn't burned up the sheets once they stripped off the clothes that set them apart.

Jessica had promised to meet him in the lobby so he didn't have to go up to her floor. Most likely so he wouldn't embarrass her—not because of how he looked, but because, hey, he was her big brother, and it was sort of his job. He stuffed his hands into his pockets and waited until he heard the sound of stilettos on tile.

Only he knew that sound, and it wasn't from his little sister.

Hair rising on the back of his neck, he turned, his smirk in place. Well, hell, it seemed today might just be his lucky day.

"Ashlynn."

CHAPTER 3

*A*shlynn had to be seeing things because there was no way her one-night stand could be standing in the middle of her company's front lobby. She'd left Jax sleeping in his Atlanta hotel room bed, all naked and roughed up from their sexcapades the night before, and she hadn't looked back.

Okay, that was a total lie since he'd been the primary focus of her thoughts and dreams since she walked out of that room, but she'd been doing a pretty darn good job of lying to herself since then.

Now that was all out the window because, *dear God,* the man was sex on a stick.

Inked and bearded sex on a stick.

And right in front of her.

"Did you follow me?" The words came out as a whispered snap, and she held back a wince. She hadn't known what she planned to say if she ever saw him again, but those particular words weren't the right ones. Not when Jax's smirk fell off his face, and his eyes narrowed at her.

"I was going to say it was damn good to see you, but maybe I should have asked if *you* were following *me*." He ran a hand over his beard, and Ashlynn wanted to cover her face with her hands.

She wasn't handling this right and was beyond flustered. Ashlynn Kelly did *not* get flustered. She was the one who made others quake in their boots. She was always the one in control.

That's what made Jax so dangerous.

And she didn't even know his last name.

She raised her chin and did her best to keep from drawing attention to herself. She didn't need gossip within her company about her, not if she wanted to keep doing what she was.

"I didn't follow you," she said softly. "I work here, Jax. I was just surprised to see you. What are you doing here?"

"Here as in Denver? I live here. Here as in this building? My little sister is an intern, and I'm taking her to lunch." He frowned at her. "Small world," he whispered.

She swallowed hard, remembering the way the heat of his whispered words felt against her skin. She couldn't let him do this to her, not here. Not now. Maybe not ever. He was supposed to be her one-night stand. Then something he'd said clicked.

"Your sister works here? She's an intern?" Ashlynn tried to remember every face that was hired, but they'd just gone through a few new interns, and she hadn't met everyone yet. Not all the new hires worked under her, but many did, and if one was related to Jax...well, it might not be the best idea to keep talking with him.

Jax's smile went soft as he spoke of his sister. "Yeah, just started a couple of weeks ago. We're proud."

"We?" she blurted and could have slapped herself.

Jax snorted. "Our mom. And me. Jessica's a bit younger than I am, so I feel like I helped raise her, even though she pretty much did most things on her own. She's a go-getter that way."

Ashlynn tried to keep her brain on the conversation, but she kept flashing back to her night with Jax. It had been the single most impulsive thing she'd ever done in her life, and now he was here, right in front of her, as if fate were taunting her decisions.

"Jax?"

Ashlynn turned to see a young brunette with a cautious smile walk up to them. She wore a nice suit with a skirt and sensible heels that still had a bit of fashion to them. Her hair was up in a cute bun at the base of her neck, and Ashlynn didn't see a hint of ink or piercings anywhere except her small hoop earrings. If it weren't for the eyes, Ashlynn wouldn't have known that Jessica and Jax were siblings, but the eyes spoke volumes.

She turned as Jax smiled widely at his sister. "There you are, runt," he said with that typical big brother attitude as he held out his arms.

Jessica glanced at Ashlynn before rolling her eyes and going in for a hug. Jax kissed his little sister's forehead, giving her a tight squeeze before he pulled back and shook his head.

"You grew up."

Jessica sighed. "You saw me four days ago." She turned and held out her hand. "Hi, I'm Jessica Reagan."

Ashlynn took the younger woman's hand and gave it a quick shake. "Nice to meet you, I'm Ashlynn Kelly. I don't think we've met, correct?"

Jessica shook her head. "No, I'm in another department, but I've seen you on my floor. I think you were out of town at a conference this past week when introductions were made."

That made sense, and Ashlynn nodded. Of course, she'd met Jax while at that conference and then had sweaty, filthy sex with the man, so things were just a tad more complicated than the other woman knew.

Jessica looked between Jax and Ashlynn with a weird look on her face, as if she were dying to ask how they knew each other but was holding back by only the barest of threads.

Ashlynn cleared her throat, needing to get out of this situation quickly before she couldn't look at herself in the morning. "Have fun at your lunch. I have a meeting." She gave Jessica a nod before barely glancing at Jax—she wasn't sure what she would do if she stared at him for too long.

Jax just gave her a knowing smile before nodding. "Enjoy your day," he whispered, and Ashlynn took off. She didn't run toward the elevator, but it was damn close. She heard Jessica whisper quickly to her brother and had a feeling it was about her, so she kept her chin up and did her best to ignore it.

Ashlynn would *not* see Jax again. There was just no way it could work, and she'd already told herself she didn't have time for men. Today was just a coincidence. Nothing more.

And if she kept telling herself that, she just might believe it.

A FEW HOURS LATER, MOST OF THE REST OF THE company had gone home, and Ashlynn had just watched a spectacular sunset from her corner office. Of course, she'd merely glanced at it since she had around four hundred things left to do on her checklist, but she'd noticed it, which was far better than most days.

Yes, she was a workaholic, but at least she was aware of it—something that couldn't be said for most of her friends and coworkers.

And though, yes, her mind was on work and finalizing the deal she'd made in Atlanta, that wasn't the only thing she was thinking about. No, it was the *other* event that had happened in Georgia that occupied far more of her thoughts than was healthy.

Jax.

He lived in Denver.

He'd been in her building that afternoon.

His sister *worked* with her.

And though she'd left him in the lobby without a look back, she had a feeling that wasn't the end—no matter how much trouble doing anything more would be.

With a sigh, she rubbed the back of her neck and frowned at the numbers in front of her. If they were starting to blur this early in her evening of work, she should probably go home and eat something so she could work some more. She'd been smart that morning since she hadn't been able to sleep the night before—thanks to naked dreams of Jax and that beard of his—and had put some food in her Crock-Pot. When she got home, she'd have a perfect chicken, potato, and veggie medley waiting for her.

At that thought, her stomach grumbled, and she saved her file before closing out her programs. Screw it. Between thoughts of food and Jax, she couldn't focus.

She might as well get one of those things since she wouldn't be having Jax tonight.

Or ever, she reminded herself. She wouldn't be having Jax ever.

"Knock, knock, princess."

Her head shot up so quickly she almost fell back in her chair. "Jax?" she breathed, then cleared her throat. "What are you doing here? How did you get into my office?" And why did she keep accusing him of things when he flustered her?

Jax tilted his head, and his hair fell over her eyes. "It's late, and there aren't that many people in the building. Your assistant, Neil, let me in when I told him who I was." He raised a brow. "The guy seemed to grin at the introduction before letting me back on his way out."

She was going to kill her assistant, well not really because he saved her life daily, but still. She'd deny him his favorite creamer or something. She hadn't meant to blurt out what she'd done with Jax in Atlanta, but she could never hide things from Neil—not when it mattered. The man seemed to be a matchmaking fiend, and it would annoy her, except he was happy with not one, but *two* people—a man and a woman—in his triad.

He had his happily ever after and wanted Ashlynn to have one, too.

Only she didn't have time for that.

"Neil is fired," she said simply and held back a laugh at Jax's eye roll. His sister had done the same thing earlier, and she couldn't help but think how alike they looked with that action.

"Sure, Ash, sure."

She swallowed hard and finished packing up her purse to give herself something to do with her hands. "Why are you here, Jax?"

He moved closer, and she held back a shiver as she looked down at his hands. Those hands had touched her, caressed her, had made her come with just a brush of calloused fingertips on her skin.

And she still didn't know his last name. Or his profession. She knew nothing about him, and yet here he was, in her office, in her hometown...and she didn't know what came next.

"I'm here because you are; because no matter what we said back in Atlanta, there was something between us. And I've got to think, an opportunity like this? Where we're together again out of *all* the places we could be? We can't let this chance pass us by."

She licked her lips, her breath shaky. "Why are you here, Jax?" she repeated. "What do you want from me?"

He was closer now, so close she could feel the heat of

him on her skin. He should have looked so out of place in her high-rise office, yet for some reason, he seemed like he belonged. She wasn't sure what to think about that.

"I want you," he said simply. "I didn't have enough of you that night, and I want more of you now. Anything you can give, Ash. Anything."

She swallowed hard and tried to get her emotions under control. "You didn't know who I was when you saw me on the street," she whispered. "Didn't know I'd be here today."

He kissed her softly, just a brush of lips. "I want to get to know you, Ash. Let me take you out to dinner, let me see who the real Ash is. You can see who I am, too."

She shook her head. "I..."

"Ash...don't say no. I'll listen if you do, but I don't want you to say no."

"I meant to say no because I don't want to go out. I have food in my Crock-Pot at home." She winced at that, and he grinned.

"My executive cooking in a Crock-Pot? That's perfect. Just tells me you know your time is valuable. So...is there enough for two?"

She let out a soft laugh. "Yeah, Jax, there should be enough food for you. I have no idea what I'm doing, but I just hope it's the right thing."

He kissed her. "I hope it's right, too, because it *feels*

right. But if we're wrong? Then we'll be wrong together. Okay?"

She leaned forward and ran her hand through his beard. "Okay."

"So, do you like working at Montgomery Ink?" she asked as they did dishes together. It was weird having a man in her space and sharing chores with him, but not as weird as it could have been if it were anyone other than Jax. For some reason, he just *fit*. That probably should have worried her more than it did, but at the moment, she'd just go with the flow—something she didn't normally do.

Jax leaned against the front of the sink and nodded. "It's a good fit, I think. I like my co-workers and the clients. Sure, there are still some people that come in and annoy me, but that's any job."

Ashlynn nodded. "Tell me about it."

"And you like being a CFO? I don't know your business day in and out, but I know enough to understand you're a big deal." He winked. "A sexy big deal, but I'll refrain from saying that in front of others if you want."

She laughed then, wondering how she could be so at ease with someone she barely knew. Yes, she knew Jax *intimately*, but she was only starting to know the man beneath the ink—and she liked him.

"I love my job," she answered once she stopped laughing, though she still had a smile on her face. "I work too hard, and I know that I should scale back and delegate, but I love what I do so much that it's sometimes hard."

"If you hated it, it would be another matter, no? Working at a place you hate drains you, makes you regret the decisions you make, even if they were the only ones you could."

There was something in his voice that made her pause, and she set her towel down on the counter. "Jax?"

He shook his head. "I worked for some bad people in Atlanta. Didn't mean to, but my old boss was a crook who had the worst kinds of connections. Once I could get out though, I did. I was a stupid kid who needed a job and had to stay because I thought I owed him." He turned to her then, and they stood face-to-face. "I was an idiot, but I'm not now. I work with great people and love my job. I'm staying in Denver long-term and don't plan on going back to any place that treats me like shit or to people who think they own me." He shrugged, and she knew there was more to his story.

"You can tell me more, if you want," she said softly. "You're a good man, Jax. You saved my life when you could have just stood back and protected yours. Plus, any man who makes sure his partner comes at least twice before he does is a good guy in my book." She winked as she said it, and Jax chuckled.

"Any man who *doesn't* make his partner come like that isn't a man I want to know." He reached forward and brushed his knuckle along her jaw. "I'm glad we found each other again, Ash."

She swallowed hard, forcing herself not to move into his touch. "Me, too."

"Now I can leave after I kiss you if you want, and we can take this slow. But, Ash? I want to taste you again. And if you want me, I'll make sure you come at least twice before I sink into you again."

She chuckled with him and let herself lean closer. "I don't want you to leave. I don't know what we're doing, but I don't want it to end."

He brushed his lips over hers, his beard softly scratching her chin in the best way possible—hell, she could get used to that. "Let me take you to the bedroom, princess."

She knew she was probably making a mistake, but she did the only thing she could at that moment. She went up on her tiptoes since she'd taken off her heels when they walked in and kissed him hard in answer.

He groaned and hoisted her, rucking up her skirt around her thighs so she could wrap her legs around his waist. She knew she'd probably torn a seam, but damn if she cared right then. She'd have thought being with him in her home would be different, that it wouldn't feel quite the same as when she'd been playing with fire and the unknown in Atlanta.

She would have been wrong.

Since the layout of her place wasn't that hard to figure out, Jax found her bedroom in no time. He sucked on her neck as he lowered her to the bed, her body arching into him, craving him. Somehow, they'd twisted so she was on her back and they kept their mouths on each other even as they stripped off their clothes, leaving them naked and twined together, his rigid cock pressed hard against her belly.

"I need you," she panted. She'd never needed anyone before, but right then, she had to have Jax inside her, over her, *with* her.

He smiled sleepily even as his eyes burned with desire. "Then you can have me." His fingers trailed over her spine before resting on her butt to give it a squeeze. "You're fucking beautiful, Ash. Inside and out."

She ducked her head, a blush heating her skin. "Jax."

He rolled them over once more and reached between them, sliding his fingers over her folds. "You're wet for me."

"That seems to be a perpetual problem when I'm around you," she teased, her breath going choppy when he circled her clit with his thumb.

"That's good to hear," he growled before sliding down her body and pressing his mouth against her.

She let out a gasp as he licked and sucked, using his fingers in unison with that tongue of his. And when he curved his fingers in just the right way, she came, her body shaking as she called out his name. Her eyes were still closed as she came down from her orgasm when he turned her over onto her belly, and she heard the sound of a condom wrapper.

"I'm going to fuck you just like this, princess. With your legs close together and your ass sticking up just so. You ready for me?"

In answer, she wiggled her hips, and he groaned before giving her a quick slap. "Jax."

"Ash," he panted before slowly sliding into her. He stretched her just right, the angle just different enough that he went deeper than he had before and yet because her legs were squeezed together, she knew her inner walls were tightening even more.

"Perfection," he growled, his hand on her hip as he thrust in and out of her. "I could stay inside you forever."

Forever.

That should have scared her since she'd only just met the man, but for some reason, she didn't want to run away in fear. Forever was just a word, after all. They were only having fun. Then she came around him, and he shouted her name, and all thoughts of whatever they were, of what they could be, fled her mind in a rush of sweet ecstasy.

Soon, she found herself wrapped around him, her body shaking against his. "Wow."

He chuckled against her temple. "Wow, indeed." His hands ran over her body lazily, as if he couldn't help but touch her. She liked it—maybe a little too much.

She was about to say something when his phone beeped from the floor, and he cursed. "What is it?"

He shook his head. "I know that tone. Give me a sec." He kissed her hard before moving to get off the bed. He walked naked around the edge of the mattress and bent over to pick up his cell from where he'd dropped it. His brows furrowed as he read the screen, and she sat up, pulling the throw that had been on top of the bed over her body so she wouldn't end up sitting there naked and confused.

"What is it?" she asked, not sure what to feel, what to think. They'd just had sex again, and yet she knew it hadn't been just sex—not when she'd started to feel something she probably shouldn't. But she had no idea what he was feeling, and now she wasn't sure she would get to find out.

"I need to go," he said gruffly as he stuffed his legs into his boxer briefs and then jeans. "I'm sorry, princess."

She could practically feel the icy exterior she wore like a shield slide over her at that moment. "I understand."

He cursed under his breath and walked to her,

cupping her face with his hand before kissing her hard. "No, you don't, and I'm sorry for that. I'm going to write my number on that whiteboard I saw on your fridge, but then I need to head out and deal with something. But I don't want to end things. I'm not leaving for good. Got me, Ash?"

"If you need to go, then go. It's not like we're serious." She knew she was just saying these things because she was scared, but she still hated the words that came out of her mouth. "It's no big deal."

He kissed her again, running his hand over her jaw. "Yeah, it is. And I'm sorry I have to leave. But I want to see you again."

"We'll see," she said honestly. Because she wasn't sure. She'd told herself she didn't have time for a man, and she didn't. She'd had work that needed to be done when she came home but hadn't done it because she was spending time with Jax. He had his own complications and life, and she wasn't sure how she fit into it all. A relationship wasn't a good idea, and if she were smart, she wouldn't look at his phone number when he left, and she'd push Jax from her thoughts altogether.

And though she was an intelligent woman, she wasn't sure she could be smart in this.

"Goodbye, Ash," he whispered. "But not forever."

She pressed her lips together and nodded, confused and unsure about what to do. Jax sighed and picked up the rest of his things before leaving her in her bedroom, naked, sated, and alone.

It didn't make sense that she was so confused by this man. She barely knew him. The problem was, she liked the things she did know. A lot. The safe thing to do would be to stay away from Jax and any complications that came from a relationship with him.

So why did Ashlynn want to dance with danger instead?

CHAPTER 4

*J*ax wanted to throw his phone at the wall and watch it shatter, but not only did he not have the money for that, he knew it wouldn't solve anything. Sammy had been texting him threats since the night before when Jax was with Ashlynn and hadn't stopped. He'd thought he left all that behind in Atlanta, but he should have known Sammy would never let go.

Jax was well and truly fucked.

Sammy was still in Atlanta, thankfully, but he was hurting for money and threatening to hurt Jessica if Jax didn't come back to the shop and work. It didn't make any fucking sense; there were other tattoo artists in the damn city, but no one was stupid enough to work for

Sammy anymore, and that meant Jax's old boss was in deep shit with the mob.

The damn mob.

Jax didn't know how his life had come to this, but he was done with it. He'd left his old home behind and had thought he'd start a new life out here, but the past kept coming back for him. It had even interrupted his time with Ashlynn, and he hated himself for it. He'd never forget the insecurity he saw on her face when he left. They hadn't made any real promises to each other, but damn if he didn't want to make them to her. He liked her, wanted her, and saw himself with her beyond a few short hours in bed.

He just hoped she saw the same in him. Yet with all the things he had going on in his life right now, he wasn't sure he'd be good for her. He was just a tattoo artist with a crap past, and she was the brilliance behind a multi-million-dollar company with a future so bright it was almost startling.

They weren't compatible on paper, yet Jax had felt something different when he was with her.

He just hoped she would call.

She had to call, damn it.

"Jax, do you have that other notebook you were using?" Austin asked from his station. "You wanted to show me that dragon, right?" The other man looked tired, but considering he'd had his own kids plus a few of his nieces and nephews over for the night so the rest of the adults could have a night out, Jax didn't blame the guy for looking like he needed four cups of coffee.

Jax rolled his shoulders and looked down at the stack of books in front of him before cursing. "Must have left it in my car. I'll go out and get it." Austin didn't need to double-check his work, but Jax had wanted the advice anyway since it wasn't the easiest design.

"You doing okay today?" Sloane asked.

"Yeah, you've seemed in your own world this morning," Derek added from Sloane's side.

Jax shook his head. "Some shit from my old shop keeps coming back, but I'm ignoring it. Hopefully, it will go away."

Austin raised a brow. "Think that'll actually work."

Jax shrugged. "Not sure what else to do so, yeah, it better work." He grabbed his keys and lifted his chin towards the other guys. "I'll be right back with that notebook." Yeah, he was changing the subject, sue him. He didn't know what to say anyway.

He'd just made it out of the back door and into the private parking lot for Montgomery Ink employees and family when large hands gripped his shoulders and slammed him into the brick wall of the tattoo shop.

"Shit," he grunted, trying to fight off his attackers. His keys fell from his hands, and he kicked out, but he was no match for *three* large men who looked to be bruisers, rather than mere muggers. "What the hell?"

"Sammy owes the boss money, asshole, and since he's not paying, you will," the biggest one growled. Though *biggest* was a bit of a misnomer since they were each huge. It wasn't until Jax saw the glint of a knife in one of the man's hands that he froze.

Jesus Christ, this couldn't be happening.

"I don't work for Sammy anymore," Jax said calmly— or at least as calm as he could considering he was being held at knifepoint by three goons.

"He says differently. He tells us that you're moonlighting and not paying him so we can't get our cut."

That goddamn bastard. Jax didn't say that aloud, but he screamed it in his head. He just prayed that these guys were only focusing on him, though, and not his family. Icy dread snaked down his spine at the thought of his mother or Jessica or *Ash* getting hurt because of his old boss.

"I don't work for him anymore. If you want your money, then get it from him. He's the one who works with y'all." Jax never had, and never would.

"Maybe we should make an example of you anyway," one of the guys whispered. "Teach Sammy a lesson."

Jax swallowed hard, trying to keep cool. "Sammy doesn't give a shit about me. You won't be getting your money at all if you hurt me. Find Sammy and get what you're owed. I'm not that man." He'd never been, no matter how hard his old life had tried to make him be.

The main goon tilted his head and studied him. "You know…Sammy has been flapping his gums for a while now. Maybe we should pay him another visit."

Shit.

"Is there a problem out here?" Austin asked from right outside the door, Sloane and Derek right beside him.

The goons dropped Jax quickly, the knife sliding back into whatever pocket it had come out of. One day, the adrenaline might dissipate from his system, but Jax didn't think that day would be anytime soon.

"We're just talking to our old friend out here," the main goon said smoothly.

"Seems like he doesn't want to be talked to," Sloane said just as simply. Jax's three friends didn't move, but they looked damn intimidating with all their ink and muscle. Things couldn't escalate, though. Jax couldn't let it because his friends weren't armed, but he had a feeling all the guys from Atlanta were.

The main guy held up his hands. "We were just heading out." He looked over at Jax. "Stay out of trouble."

Jax gave them a tight nod, his body as tense as ever, but as the guys from his past walked away, he had an odd feeling that they might be leaving for good. They'd threatened him, sure, but they hadn't actually hurt him like they could have. And, hell, they had to know by now that he didn't have a damn thing for them. He'd never been part of that business and had made damn sure that everyone knew that. He just hoped that would be enough. As for Sammy? Well, Sammy had made his own mess and would have to deal with the consequences.

Jax was done. He held back a wince as he turned to Sloane, Austin, and Derek. Well, he hoped he wasn't done completely because he hadn't meant for anyone to know exactly what he'd gone through before he came to Denver.

"I have a friend I'm going to call to make sure they don't come back," Sloane said softly before heading back into the shop, and Jax's eyes widened.

Austin shrugged. "We have friends in good places sometimes. Now get that damn notebook and come back inside. We'll talk about what happened later with Maya because if she hears about this from anyone else, there'll be hell to pay."

Jax would have laughed, but he didn't have it in him at the moment. Maya was a force to be reckoned with, and you did not mess with Austin's sister. That was probably why Jax liked her so much.

"Okay."

"We'll stay out here with you," Derek added. "Just in case."

Jax blew out a breath. "Okay." He cleared his throat. "Thank you."

In answer, Austin raised his chin, and Jax moved quickly to his car, picking up his keys from the gravel on the way. He wasn't shaking, but he was damned close. He could have died just then, and it wouldn't have been his fault. Yet, in the end, it wouldn't have mattered—not when it came to Sammy's problems.

By the time he made it back inside the shop, he was ready to sit down and find something cool to drink to help his parched tongue. What he hadn't been expecting to see was anyone in his booth.

He damn sure wasn't expecting Ashlynn in her sexy as hell high heels and stone grey skirt and jacket.

"Ash?"

She turned at the sound of his voice and widened her eyes. "Jax. Are you okay?" She rushed to him and cupped his face. "You have a cut here." Her other hand hovered over his jaw, and he winced. He hadn't felt it until she pointed it out and now it stung, but he ignored it since she was here and touching him.

"I'll be okay," he whispered, aware that the others were staring at him, but Jax didn't want to go outside to talk to her privately, not with what had just happened.

She bit her lip, looking unsure. "If you say so."

"What are you doing here, Ash?" he asked softly. "Not that I don't love seeing you."

"I wanted to see you," she whispered. "I didn't like how we left things last night. I was a little confused, and heck, I'm *still* a little confused, but I shouldn't have been so cold when you said you had to go."

He cupped her face then, loving the softness of her skin under his touch. "You weren't cold." She'd been scared, probably because they were moving so fast, and he'd understood. "I'm glad you're here."

She smiled then. "I could have called, but I wanted to see you." She cleared her throat. "So...want to go get lunch?"

He laughed then. "Lunch I can do."

"And I want to get to know you more. Not just...you know." She blushed, and Jax fell a little for her then. He wasn't ready to fall completely, but with this woman, he knew he eventually could. They needed time together, and then...well, then they'd learn each other even more.

"That sounds like a plan, princess." He kissed her softly. "You okay with the fact that I'm a tattoo artist with no degree or fancy car?" He winked. "I have a bike that you'd look fucking sexy on, though."

She rolled her eyes. "You okay that I'm kind of icy sometimes and work long hours?"

"I can work with that," he whispered before kissing her hard, pulling her so close that he knew his dick pressed into her even through all their layers of clothing. Ashlynn did that to him with a mere glance, and he *loved* it.

"Awww."

Jax didn't know which man had said it or if it was more than one of them, so he just flipped off the room even as he kept his lips on Ash.

Ashlynn pushed away and ducked under his chin. "I forgot we weren't alone."

He kissed the top of her head. "I like that you forgot."

She pulled away and frowned. "You're going to tell me why you're cut, though."

It wasn't a question, and he didn't mind. "Tonight. I promise. I'll tell you everything."

"Good," she said with a smile, and he kissed her again.

"I could get used to this," she murmured against his lips.

"Yeah? Me, too."

He kissed her once more.

He hadn't planned on Ashlynn in his life. Hell, he hadn't intended anything but freedom. But now that he had his woman, his executive in his arms, he knew he didn't mind the surprise.

Ashlynn was the best shock of his life.

And he couldn't wait to find out more.

SECOND CHANCE INK

A MONTGOMERY INK ROMANCE

From NYT bestselling author Carrie Ann Ryan comes a new romance in her Montgomery Ink series…

Tattoo artist Brandon never thought he'd see her again. He'd trained himself never to think of her or what they'd had together. It was the only way he'd been able to survive but now she's standing right in front of him and he can hardly breathe.

Lauren hadn't known he'd be part of her plans until it was too late. She'd thought he was gone from her life and memories forever. Now he's in her orbit once more and she'll have to fight to remember the girl she once was and the woman she's become.

Author Note: Second Chance Ink is a Montgomery Ink short story and a little different than what you're used to from me. It's shorter than my other novellas at only ~12,000 words. It has a complete HEA, and is perfect for a steamy evening, one-sitting read.

CHAPTER 1

BRANDON

I was having a damn fantastic day, and it had everything to do with the lovely curves in front of me. There was nothing better in life than a blank canvas of perfect, supple flesh that begged for a needle. I had prime, virgin skin laid out before me on a woman who had a high pain tolerance—one who never even moved when I had to dig a little deeper to finish shading the edges.

Yes, today was one of the good days, and the sweet mom of four who lay on her side on my table as I worked on her ribs and hips was the sole reason. She wanted a full piece that was seriously detailed and would take me more than a couple of sessions. But considering that I really liked working on her, and the art that we came up with together was pretty fantastic, I didn't mind the long hours. This is what I'd trained for, what I loved about working at Montgomery Ink.

My client, Kim, had come in with the idea of putting some of her favorite book series together in a long and complicated array that would all fit into one big piece. She was an avid romance reader and had asked every single author she wanted to be tattooed with if it was okay if she used their series logos or objects that represented them. Apparently, the authors either replied happily "yes" or had cried and said "yes." If I had the talent to be an author and someone wanted to use my work in that way, I'd have probably said yes, as well. Kim was essentially putting part of their souls on her body, and that work would remain there until the day she died. If that wasn't a symbol of her dedication and love for the authors and their work, I didn't know what was.

"How you doing, Kim?" I asked as I leaned back, stretching a bit. She might be the one with a needle in her skin, but with how much I was bending over today, I'd probably end up just as sore. There was a reason one of my favorite artists outside of the shop wore corsets while he worked.

"I'm okay." She smiled sleepily at me, and I couldn't help but grin. She was seriously the perfect client. Getting a tattoo didn't always put people in their unique subspace or give them a high, but Kim dropped right in after only a few minutes of wincing. If *I* could do that, I'd probably have a lot more ink than I did.

As it was, my entire left arm and side were ink-free, as was most of my right arm. I had a full back piece, and most of my chest and thighs were covered, but I hadn't figured out exactly what I wanted to do for my sleeves yet. Considering that the old adage of never trusting a tattoo artist without ink was something most people listened to, I ended up showing off my back a lot. My boss, Maya, said I should just tattoo shirtless at this point, even if it wasn't exactly up to code. But I assumed that was just a joke. At least I hoped it was since if I actually showed up without a shirt, she'd probably kick my ass.

Not that I ever really knew with Maya or her brother Austin, who also owned the shop. They tended to take sarcasm to the next level—just one more reason why I loved working here. I fit right in. I figured it would take another few years before I reached the level of sarcasm the Montgomerys and their ilk had attained, though. I didn't mind. I'd spent the past few years being a journeyman of sorts, going from shop to shop, honing my craft and learning from some of the best artists out there. I wanted to learn exactly what it meant to be a tattoo artist beyond the craze that the media seemed to show these days. I loved drawing and figuring out exactly what

I wanted my character sketches to turn into in the end. But it wasn't until I got my first tattoo at the tender age of seventeen—after lying and saying that I was actually twenty—that I knew exactly what I wanted to be when I grew up. It took over ten years of honing my craft and going from place to place until I finally found my home at Montgomery Ink.

"If you're sure," I finally said after letting Kim relax a bit. "Then let's keep going." The others around us were talking and working, but I focused my attention solely on Kim and her ink. I wanted to do a damn good job for her, and to do that, I had to put any distractions and worries from my mind.

Another hour passed, and I knew I was done for the day, at least with Kim. I needed to refill my energy, and I could tell that Kim was starting to feel it. She'd been lying in the same position for hours now, and while she might be a trooper, everyone had his or her limit. We'd found hers.

"Okay, that's it for the day," I said, sitting up and trying not to wince at my own aches and pains. I wasn't even thirty yet, but my body was feeling it. I'd have to do some yoga and stretching when I got home to make sure I didn't end up hurting myself like some of the other artists I knew. Thankfully, the crew at Montgomery Ink was good about taking care of their bodies and their skills. Maya had even been talking about doing group yoga sessions, but I was pretty sure Austin would nix that idea. There was group bonding, and then there was group stretching and groaning. That might be a little too much for us.

"I think you're right," Kim said, wincing a little. "I wish we could have done it in one go, but I'm pretty sure I want a bath."

I raised a brow. "No baths. You know that." We went over aftercare instructions as I helped her stand so she could see how much we'd gotten done. The fact that she had happy tears in her eyes told me that no matter how much pain a tattoo caused or how many stretches I'd have to do later, I was doing exactly what I should be.

Kim scheduled her next appointment with me, and I went back to my station to clean up. My brain was still on her ink rather than anything around me, so it took me a few minutes to realize that Callie and Derek were trying to get my attention.

I blinked then rolled my eyes since the two of them appeared to be doing some weird version of an Irish jig. Callie had the leg movements down but was waving her arms in the air like one of those dudes in front of a car dealership. Derek was sort of moving his feet, but it was almost a mix of a two-step and a jig. I knew they could dance when they actually tried, but whatever the hell they were doing now was so ridiculous, I couldn't help but crack up.

"I thought you were going to zone out *forever*," Callie said, adding emphasis to the last word so she sounded like a teenager instead of the mother of two she was. I still couldn't quite believe the woman in front of me already had two kids and was married to a very big and powerful man. She was around my age, but how she had so much energy...I had no idea.

"It wasn't forever," I said, rolling my eyes before going back to cleaning up. I could focus on the conversation and finish up at the same time but, apparently, my mind had been a little too into the latter when they were trying to get my attention.

"Just a little bit of forever." Callie came to my side and helped me with the last of the sanitizing while Derek leaned over the half wall that separated each station. "I saw what you did for Kim. It's freaking amazing. I can't wait to see what it looks like when you're finished."

"Yeah, you're pretty good," Derek said, laughter in his eyes. "I mean, I guess you qualify as talented or some shit. But, whatever."

"Don't you dare throw that, Brandon," Maya shouted as she walked into the building. "I have no idea what it is since I can't see your hand, but I know you." She winked as she said it, and I grinned back.

"I only throw things when you're not looking," I said, stepping out of my station. "I thought you were staying home today."

She shrugged. "Jake and Border wanted a guys' day with the kids, even though I explained that the baby is a girl even if her big brother isn't. But they didn't care what I said. So instead of staying home and hiding in the office while they do whatever they do, I figured I'd come here and get some paperwork done."

"So maternity leave is a bust, then?" Derek said, opening his arms so Maya could give him a hug. I did the same, and she leaned into my hold. We were a pretty tight-knit group and were constantly hugging. To the outside world, a bunch of big, tattooed and pierced guys being affectionate with each other probably sounded like fiction, but they didn't know my friends. It helped that the women who worked at Montgomery Ink never let the guys forget that hugging was okay.

"I don't want to talk about it."

I gave Maya a look, and she sighed. "Maya. Talk to Uncle Brandon."

Derek snorted, and Callie just laughed, but both of them stayed silent otherwise. I could see the worry on their faces for their friend, as well. Maya wrapped her arms around her middle, looking far more vulnerable than I'd ever seen her. She was one of the toughest women I knew and took no shit from anyone. She was married to *two* men and faced the world as if anyone who came at them could fuck right off. Yet, right now, she didn't have that strength I was used to in her eyes. It worried me.

"I just hate being away from the babies. And I hate being away from my shop. And if it made sense to have children constantly around needles and people coming in to get tattoos and piercings, I would bring them in. Hell, there's so many kids attached to the crew here, we should just open up a daycare."

Callie wrapped her arm around Maya's waist. "Didn't some of your other family create daycare for their business?"

Maya nodded, and Brandon remembered that of Maya's seven siblings, a few of them worked in the construction arm of the Montgomery businesses. And because every single Montgomery in the area seemed to have procreated at least once in the past three years— sometimes twice—there were a lot of babies who needed a safe place to stay during the day while Mom and Dad worked.

"It works for them because they have the space in their building for a full-on Montgomery daycare center. And I know I can just bring my kids there. I have in the past when Jake or Border couldn't be with them because of their jobs, but it isn't the same. I can't see my kids, and I want to, but I have to work. I can't even say 'have to' at this point because I love my job. I love working here. I need to draw and work on other people's dreams, but I'm having a typical mommy moment where I feel guilty that I'm not home with my babies. It's silly, even though I know it's not."

We did our best to soothe Maya and told her that no matter how many times she left her children with very qualified babysitters or her cousins and the children of close friends, it didn't make her any less of a mother. Even as I said the words, I wished there was something I could do to make it better. Other than Derek and me, every other artist at the shop had at least one child. There'd been a huge boom of marriages and babies recently. Somehow, Derek and I had ducked the blast.

I didn't have kids...hadn't been blessed with that yet. I'd spent the past decade or so hopping from bed to bed— man or woman—because I hadn't found the one person for me. I'd been enjoying living my life where my only commitment was work. I wasn't ready to settle down. I suppose it's the typical life of a bisexual man who isn't quite ready for the next stage of his life.

"Why can't you have your kids here every once in a while?" My voice cut into the others' conversations, and they turned to look at me.

"What?" Maya asked.

"It's not like you work on tattoos day in and day out when you're in this building. None of us do. Some days, we're just here to sketch or work the front if Autumn isn't here." Autumn was one of Maya's sisters-in-law who worked the front desk for them and scheduled appointments when the rest of them were too busy. "And I'm not saying everyone should bring in their kids, but, Maya, you own this place. On days when you're here to just do paperwork and feel like you can actually do that and hold your baby at the same time…why not bring the newborn? I know your oldest probably needs a little more room to spread out, and the daycare situation with the rest of your family is probably the better option there. But I, for one, am not going to hold you back if you want to bring your kid in. And if you ever need a moment and can't hold your child, I'm pretty sure there are enough arms in here open to holding that very adorable baby of yours."

Maya's eyes filled with tears, and I stiffened, worried that I'd somehow upset her. Not only was it dangerous for me if I upset Maya because she could kick my ass, but she was also married to two very big men that could take me without blinking. And not in a fun way.

"That is so sweet, Brandon. Maybe I will bring the baby in. It's not like we need to open up a whole daycare center or anything. Not only do we not have the space, but having the kids at Montgomery Inc. is actually a better deal in the long run. That way, they won't grow up alone. I just suck at this whole separation thing."

"You are not alone," Callie said, hugging her friend close.

"You do realize how many times Hailey and I have

wanted to bring Oliver in with us, right?" Sloane was married to the café owner next door, and they had recently adopted their son, Oliver. "The fact that he can hang out with your kids during the day makes the idea that he's not in our arms while we're both working okay."

The rest of them started talking about various milestones in their children's lives, and I zoned out slightly. Before long, Derek and I went back to our stations to get to work. It was weird to think that I was somehow falling behind when it came to my friends' lives and the steps they were taking in them. When I first started at the tattoo shop, everyone was single. Then Austin married Sierra, Maya married Jake and Border, Callie married Morgan, Sloane married Hailey, Blake married Jake's brother Graham, and even our newest hire, Jax, just married his girl, Ashlynn.

Though I had a feeling Jax wouldn't be the last one walking down the aisle—or at least making a commitment. Derek had been acting weird recently. He'd been secretive, and no matter how hard my friend tried to hide what was going on with him, I *knew* it had to do with a woman. Only one thing in the world could put that look on my friend's face. It had to be the woman he never spoke of.

Of course, I really couldn't say anything to Derek about it because I didn't pry when it came to relationships or heartbreak. I had hidden my own for so long that it was any wonder people thought I took anything seriously beyond my art. Somehow, I was the one people came to for advice and relationships—along with Derek. Yet neither of us were honest about who we'd loved and lost. I didn't know Derek's secrets, but when he didn't know I was looking, I saw the same things on his face that I hid from others.

But that was enough thinking about that. I hadn't thought of Lauren and how she'd left without a word for so long, I'd almost forgotten what she looked like. And *that* was a complete lie. I would never forget the warmth in her eyes. The long, chestnut hair that slid over my body as she took me into herself. I'd never forget the feel of her beside me, or how she felt in my heart. Not until the day I died.

And because I didn't like thinking about her anymore, didn't like the feelings that came when I remembered that I had no idea where she was or what she was doing, I took out my sketchpad and started drawing. It was easier to get lost in the work than the memories. At least that's what I told myself and how I spent the past six years becoming the artist I now was. The others had gone back to work, their clients walking in for their appointments while Maya went back to the office to get paperwork done.

I was so focused on my sketchpad that I didn't notice the bell on the top of the door ring until I heard a familiar voice that should've been locked in my memory instead of coming from right in front of me.

I froze, my stomach clenching and my back tightening as if someone had ripped through my skin and gripped my spine.

It couldn't be. After all these years, it *couldn't* be. Maybe it was because I'd thought of her. I'd conjured her voice up out of nowhere. Because there was no way the lost love of my life, my Lauren, could be here.

But as I looked up at the front desk where Derek was talking to a beautiful woman with long, chestnut hair, I knew I wasn't imagining things.

My past had come back, and instead of running away or hiding or saying something that could possibly make the situation okay, I growled.

"What are you doing here, Lauren?"

I hadn't meant to say that. I hadn't meant to sound like such an asshole but, apparently, seeing the love of your life who ran away without a word after an event that should've brought a couple closer meant that being a nice guy went straight out the window.

"You. You're here." She breathed the words rather than truly saying them, and I had a feeling she hadn't known I was here. Her face went so white, I swore there wasn't an ounce of blood left in it.

The place had gone quiet, and Derek looked between the two of us as if trying to figure out exactly what was going on. It wasn't as if I could help him because I had no clue what was going on either.

"You're here."

She blinked, opened her mouth to say something, and then did the one thing she'd always been good at. She ran.

This time, I did the one thing I should've done all those years ago...I followed.

CHAPTER 2

LAUREN

I couldn't catch my breath. Why couldn't I catch my breath? He shouldn't affect me like this. It had been years. Why couldn't I catch my breath?

I ran from the tattoo shop as if the Devil's own hellhounds were on my tail, yet I had no idea why. I wasn't that lost young woman anymore. I shouldn't have run. But it had been so unexpected to see him, to have that blast from my past thrown in my face as if no time had passed at all.

Yet everything had changed since the last time I saw him, my heart in his hands, and tears running down my cheeks. I wasn't the same woman. And from the hard edge in his eyes, I knew he wasn't the same man anymore either. As I thought the words *man* and *woman*, I couldn't help but think that we were more boy and girl back then.

Being in your early twenties, making big decisions and falling in love even when you didn't understand the depths of the horrors and complications of the real world didn't make you an adult. We may have had some of the worst parts of our lives thrown at us at a young age, but we were still so young.

I had only run a block before I finally slowed down, realizing that people were staring, and I was acting like a lunatic. We might be in downtown Denver where people running for the bus or even to Starbucks for that matter wasn't anything new, but I had a feeling the look on my face said that my haste had nothing to do with being late and everything to do with running away.

A hand clenched my shoulder, and I froze, my heart racing. I should've known he would follow. He would've followed before if I'd given him the chance. But I'd been so scared that I hadn't. Now, I knew I needed to be an adult and turn around to face the boy I left behind, the one who was now the man I hadn't thought to ever see again.

"Lauren."

I knew that deep voice. I'd heard that voice whispering in my ear and screaming my name over and over and over again. I'd heard that voice trying to soothe me as I broke, and joking with me as I grew. I'd fallen in love with that voice and the boy who came with it; yet I wasn't sure I could turn to face it now.

But I wasn't that scared, young woman any longer, so I rolled my shoulders back, knocking off his hand as I did so, and turned to see the boy I had left behind. It was strange that I called him titles like that, things that held meaning yet didn't encompass the full breadth of the man he was or the person he had been. In my head, I couldn't call him anything that might start to mean something more. But I had to be strong. I had been through hell and back, and I could use a name. There was power in that, and I could hold that power.

"Brandon." He looked slightly different than the last time I had seen him before I walked into that tattoo shop earlier, but he still had the same air of the person I once knew. His hair was longer, nearly brushing his shoulders now with those natural highlights I had once coveted. Seriously, how could a man look so pretty and yet sexy at the same time? He was slender, but he was all muscle. I could see tattoos down his right arm but none on his left. In fact, I didn't see too many tattoos at all, which really wasn't that much different than before. Considering his job, I would've thought he would have gotten more by now.

"Lauren, you're here." His words echoed my own from when I first saw him and had no clue what to say. I knew he had to be in the same boat as I was. Confused and yet thrust back into a past we couldn't deny. He cleared his throat, and I couldn't help but look at his face. I'd missed that face—more than I cared to admit. "I honestly can't believe you're standing here in front of me. How did you find me? Or maybe that's a little too self-centered. Is it just a coincidence that you happen to be in Denver again, standing in front of me after walking into the place where I work? I should say, what are you doing here? How have you been? Where the hell did you go?"

I shook my head. "I didn't know you would be there. I'd heard good things about the place and wanted to go in and maybe make an appointment if I could gather the courage. I really didn't know that you worked there. And as for everything else you just asked? Standing here on a street corner where people are looking at us as they pass by is probably not the best place to have this conversation. And because I'm still shocked that I even saw you in the first place, I don't even know if we should have that conversation at all. It's been a long time since we saw each other, Brandon. Maybe we should just let the past live where it needs to: in the past."

Brandon's jaw tightened but I stood still, not wanting to break the moment, yet not wanting to back down either. I was in this weird state of both the past and the present as they mixed together with no idea what might happen once the spell broke and I found myself standing alone in the city I left behind, wondering how the hell to take the next step.

"Come with me to my place. It's just two blocks away,

not even that. I deserve answers, Lauren. Yeah, it's been a long time, but you left without a word. And I want to know what I did. I want to know why you left and didn't say anything. Don't disregard the connection we had with each other or throw it away again by saying I don't deserve answers. Because they're a long time coming, Lauren. I loved you. And I deserve to know why you didn't love me enough to stay."

Tears stung my eyes, and I swallowed hard. I knew I had hurt him. We were so young. But there were two things I hadn't been able to tell him. Maybe he was right, maybe it was time for me to open up and actually say the words I'd been so scared to say. But he was wrong, too. I had loved him—enough to leave. I had loved him more than I'd ever thought possible, and that's why I didn't stay. But I didn't know how I would explain that to him. I could barely explain it to myself. And though it would be crazy to follow him to his apartment after not seeing him for so long, I knew that he deserved this conversation. And it wasn't one I wanted to have in public. Because I had a feeling I wasn't going to make it through without a few tears, without a few breakdowns. I hadn't broken down yet, and Brandon deserved more than stony silence.

"Okay. I'll go with you. Because you're right, we do need to talk." I was never one to believe in fate. No...that might not be true. I probably believed in it more when I was a little girl and believed in fairies, gold at the end of rainbows, and Santa. But I wasn't sure I could believe in fate and a divine destiny that would put me through everything that I had gone through.

"That was a quick change of heart, but I'm not going to take that for granted and sit here and wait for you to change your mind again. So, come on. Let's go." He held out his hand, and after a moment's hesitation, I took it, knowing that one action might change my life once again. But as with everything that had to do with Brandon, I knew change was inevitable.

"Don't you need to go back to work? Aren't they going to wonder why you just ran out of there and chased me?" I was still holding his hand as he led me down the one and a half blocks to his apartment building. It was one of the refurbished structures that Denver had just finished adding to the skyline. It hadn't been here when I lived near the city. I didn't remember exactly what building was here before but it had probably been one of the ones practically falling down with no historical value other than its age. Denver did its best to try and save everything historic in the city, but sometimes, the foundations just weren't there. I tried not to let that train of thought be symbolic in any way with what I was about to tell Brandon. But, sometimes, things were a little too on the nose.

"I'll text them once we get upstairs. If they didn't

follow me, they must have an idea what I'm doing. I'm sure they were all staring out the window and saw me talking to you. They're my friends, it's what we do."

I nodded, though I didn't truly understand. I didn't have those kinds of friends anymore, not with all the moving and healing I'd been forced to do recently. But all of that was going to change soon, darn it. Because I was back in town, and I was going to put down roots, make friends, and start a new life where I wasn't scared of everything coming at me all at once. And to start that, I was going to face the man I once loved and try to explain exactly why I ran—not once, but twice.

We made it inside his apartment on the fifth floor, but I was so nervous that I didn't really take in what it looked like. I figured if I could get through what I needed to say, I'd be able to see how his decorating styles and tastes had changed over the years.

Brandon stood in front of me as if he weren't sure what to do with himself or his hands. I didn't blame him because even though I was scared and wanted nothing more than to hide away, I also wanted to lean into his hold, bury myself in the earthy scent of him, and never let go. Attraction and sexual hunger had never been a problem between us, and from the heat in his eyes, I had a feeling I wasn't the only one thinking that.

"I need to tell you some things. I need to...*do* a lot of things."

Brandon cupped my cheek, and I licked my lips, memories of the last time he had touched me, the last time he'd held me slamming into my mind. His hand was so big and warm on my face. It made me feel as if with just one touch, all my worries could wash away. That he would protect me from anything that came at us. I knew that wasn't the case, and that no matter how strong you were, things still came at you, but with his touch, and in his hold, I could believe the impossible.

"I know we should talk, but all I want to do is kiss you. Is that wrong? God, Lauren, it's been six damn years. We're different people. Yet all I can do is try and hold myself back from crushing my mouth to yours and tasting you again. It's stupid. We need to talk, we need to figure out exactly what happened, and I know you said you have things to say. Hell, so do I. But please let me kiss you. It's like no time has passed, and yet all the time in the world. Let me kiss you, Lauren. Let me taste your lips again. Even if it's just one last time. Give me that right, give me that chance. Let me kiss you."

And because I couldn't deny Brandon anything, not even the truth, not anymore, I opened my mouth and said, "Yes. Kiss me."

Brandon pressed his lips to mine, and I was lost. I was spun right back into our first kiss, the first time we saw each other and smiled under the waning moon after our first date. I was so nervous, so young and a little unsure, but in Brandon's arms, I always felt safe and protected. Our first kiss had been hesitant, then it had grown into something far deeper, far hotter. It had taken us a couple of months to sleep together the first time because Brandon had always been good about taking care of me. But I could still taste our first kiss. And as Brandon pressed his lips to mine now, our first kiss, our next kiss, and our last kiss slammed into me, and I knew running again might not be an option anymore. It made no sense to me that after six years apart, a single kiss could change all that, but it had always been that way with Brandon. I might not believe in fate, but I had once believed in the idea that two souls could become forever entwined and wrapped around each other in a manner where distance and time could not separate them. And as romantic as that sounded, the poetic tragedy of it all made me want to cry.

But even as all those thoughts spun through my mind on an endless loop, I still could taste Brandon on my lips and my tongue. He cupped my face, tilted my head to the side, and I parted my mouth for him. His tongue tangled with mine, and I moaned. He was Brandon, exquisite and delicious, and he had once been mine.

The kiss deepened, and our bodies pressed closer together, the hard line of his erection digging into my hip. Some part of me wanted nothing more than to keep going and take this to the bedroom, strip off all our clothes, and make love as if no time had passed. As if my body and my soul hadn't been damaged. But that wasn't the case. I might have healed in certain ways, but in order to keep my strength, I needed to pull back and tell Brandon the truth. I wasn't ashamed, not anymore, but things needed to be said nonetheless.

So I pulled back and rested my hands on his so I could lower them from my face. His lips were swollen, his eyes dark, and I knew if I let him, he would keep kissing me until we were both out of breath. And because I knew that could be an inevitability, I didn't move forward.

"I've missed that. I've missed you." Brandon stuffed his hands into his pockets as if he weren't sure what to do with them. I didn't blame him. If I had pockets in my leggings, I would've done the same thing.

We stood awkwardly in front of each other, his taste on my tongue, my cheek still warm from his touch, and the past like an ocean between us even though only six inches separated us.

"Why did you leave?" Brandon hadn't given me the option to say that I had missed him as well, but that was okay. I wasn't sure I could tell him that without breaking down. It wasn't as if I could get through this day without crying anyway, though. "It wasn't because of me was it? It wasn't because we thought we had lost the baby?"

I stood there, a tear slowly rolling down my cheek as I heard the man I had once loved—possibly still loved—

telling me one of what had to be his greatest fears. Because him thinking that was one of mine.

I had broken something between us because I was scared, and though I would never forgive myself for that, what made it worse was that I had hurt the man in front of me. And now it was time that I told him why. No matter the cost.

CHAPTER 3

LAUREN

"*I* didn't leave because of you. I didn't leave because we thought we lost the baby." I knew that no matter how many other things I needed to tell him today, that was the first thing I needed to set in stone. We had been scared, together, young and possibly a little stupid. But we had been together. And when I left, it wasn't because of what we'd gone through, but rather what I refused to *put* him through.

And though I probably should've practiced what I planned to say to him, I suddenly found myself at a loss for words.

Brandon stood in front of me, not touching but so close I could feel the heat of him. "You say that, but I don't know if I can believe you. We were so scared, so *excited* about the thought of being parents, even though we were way too young to even comprehend what that meant. The fact that you turned out not to be pregnant threw us both for a loop. You left right after that, and I couldn't help but put two and two together."

I shook my head, my hands clenched into fists in front of me. "No, it wasn't like that." I let out a breath, trying to collect my thoughts. "I didn't leave without a word, you know that." It might have been six years ago, but I could at least remember how I left.

He let out a breath, though his shoulders were still visibly tense. "I remember. I remember the fact that after the pregnancy scare, we pretty much stopped talking. Then the next moment, it seemed you were moving away with your parents even though you were out of college. You left, Lauren."

"It wasn't at all like that, and you know it. After we thought I was pregnant and it turned out not to be the case, we drifted. Maybe we should've talked more, maybe we should have acted like the adults we thought we were, but we didn't. You backed away just as much as I did. Don't stand there and act as if I was the one who moved away first."

Brandon's eyes narrowed. "I loved you, Lauren. Yeah, I was scared, and a little disappointed that we weren't going to have a kid even though I knew it wasn't the right time, but I still loved you. I gave you the space I thought you needed. I didn't run away. I was just giving you space."

I bit my lower lip. "I know that now. But I didn't then. I thought you were backing away because you were scared like I was. I thought you were pulling away because you realized that having that connection, that forced ball and chain or whatever, would be too much. In retrospect, I know I overreacted, but I had a lot of other things on my plate. More than I even knew at the time."

He ran a hand through his long hair and scowled. "What are you talking about? You keep using these vague references I don't understand. If you're saying you didn't skip town after our last conversation because of the baby, then what was it?"

I could still remember standing in front of him two weeks after finding out I wasn't pregnant. I was so scared, but not for the reasons he probably thought. Not for the same reasons he thought now. I assumed he thought I was already too much for him—too much to deal with—so I said I needed time to think and then did exactly what he thought I did. I ran away. But now, I needed to explain to him that I didn't run away from *him*. The running was from the circumstances that had led me here, today.

"I had to leave." I rolled my shoulders back, meeting his gaze. "My family needed me to go with them when they moved for my dad's job because I couldn't be alone.

Not with all the doctors' visits and surgeries I needed at the time."

There, I'd said part of it. It didn't make it any easier to stomach, but at least I'd said something other than that I was sorry for breaking both of our hearts.

His eyes widened, and he took a step forward, his fingertips brushing the skin of my forearm. "What are you talking about? Surgeries? Doctors' visits? What happened, Lauren?"

"It turns out the pregnancy scare was a symptom. You and I figured out we weren't pregnant because we took, what, five pregnancy tests that were at-home kits? They were all negative, and then I got my period right after that. But it hurt more than usual and only lasted a couple days."

"I remember you always had issues with your cycle. It was why you were on the type of birth control you were, even before we met. What happened, Lauren?" he repeated.

Baring my soul to anyone was hard. Baring my soul to the man I hurt because I was afraid of what my life would become would be agony. But he deserved the truth, and I wasn't sick anymore, so maybe fate had decided that this was when I should tell him everything.

"I had ovarian cancer. I was only twenty-two, and even my doctors were surprised at how virulent it had become." If I closed my eyes, I could still imagine the stab of needles in my skin as they did test after test to figure out exactly how such a young, otherwise healthy woman could have a body trying to kill itself. Because you weren't supposed to get cancer when you were twenty-two. Ovarian cancer, breast cancer, all of those things were supposed to happen to older women who were forced to take tests and have mammograms and all of that other stuff every year because it could happen to them at any moment. And having cancer in the part of me that I had once thought made me a woman, especially right when I'd thought perhaps I could be a mother, had thrown my world off its axis. I'd since learned more about what it meant to be a woman, and what my body said about me, but at twenty-two—a sheltered twenty-two at that—my world seemed to crash down around me.

And I didn't know how to explain that to the man in front of me. Because he had seen inside of me, had touched my soul at one point, and yet that same spark wasn't there anymore. I wasn't the same girl I once was. And while on some level I understood that, I didn't know if he could.

Before I could open my mouth and say anything else, Brandon's arms were around me, holding me close to him. He ran his strong hands down my hair, my back, and clutched me to him. He kissed the top of my head, my temple, my cheek, and murmured sweet words that I knew I had heard from him before. But I couldn't quite comprehend them now because all I could do was sink into his hold and wrap my arms around his waist. I had felt like this before, I remembered: his arms and his touch like a sense of home I never knew I needed. I'd always felt safe with him, felt as if my center of gravity shifted towards him. I had forgotten that fact. I had forgotten what it felt like to be held by a man who truly cared, one who truly put his all into those he loved.

I had forgotten, but with one touch, it all came back with force.

"You healthy now? Or maybe that's too personal a question, but I need to know. Are you okay, Lauren? Dammit, I wish I had been there to help you through that. And now I sound as if your illness had something to do with me rather than the very personal thing it was. I'm so sorry, baby."

I let him hold me a few moments longer before pulling back so I could look into his eyes. He kept his hand on mine, and I didn't mind. I needed that anchor, and knew he did, too—especially because I knew I wasn't done yet.

"I'm cancer-free now. But it was really bad back then. Right when I thought you were pulling away because you were afraid of being a dad, I was finding out that I had cancer in my body that was trying to take away my life. My mom went with me to the doctor's office that day because she didn't like how pale I had been looking, and even though I was way over the age of being an adult, I have always been thankful that she was there with me. I had stage III ovarian cancer—a death sentence in some cases. But because I was young and healthy in all other aspects, they were able to aggressively attack the cancer. My parents were already planning to move to Seattle because of my dad's job, and though there were wonderful doctors here then, even cutting-edge doctors that could have helped me, there was an even better oncologist up in Seattle. So I went with my parents. Moved away from the home that I had grown up in, the home I had made for myself once I moved out, and the city that had been my own, to move into my parents' new house. It wasn't easy, and I knew in the end that I was running away from not only you but also the girl I was when I thought I had a full future ahead of me. But I think it's what I needed to do. I'm just sorry that I hurt you in the process."

He shook his head and cupped my face again. "How could you think about me at all during that? Yeah, a part of me is pissed off that I couldn't be there for you and that, somehow, you didn't trust me enough to be strong for you, but that part needs to go away. Because you being sick had nothing to do with me. And I'm just so damn sorry about everything. But you're okay now? Right?"

"Like I said, I'm cancer-free. But it wasn't without a

cost." A terrible cost that I was just now learning to live with. I just had to remember that I wasn't the same woman I once was, and that was a good thing when it came to the strength in my body and in my veins. "I had a full hysterectomy at the age of twenty-two that put me through early menopause. So, in addition to all the chemo, and radiation, and constant poking and prodding to make sure I could live, I also lost a part of myself I had truly thought I relied on to give me a sense of self."

"And you did this on your own. I always knew you were strong, Lauren. But I never knew how strong you could be." His thumb ran along my cheekbone, but I didn't lean into his touch. He wasn't mine anymore, and we weren't the same people we were. I didn't know this man, and he was only starting to learn the bare facts of who I was.

"I wasn't alone. I had my parents. Yes, maybe I should've called to tell you when and why we left town. But I was so focused on the future in front of me, and how scared I was, that I couldn't find the strength to do so. I was young, and so damn scared that I was going to die that I didn't want to bring you into that part of my life. That might have been selfish, but I thought you'd find someone else to fall in love with and have a life where you didn't have to worry about a woman who was literally dying inside."

"Jesus Christ, Lauren. How could you even think that

I would have run away from you being sick? I would've been by your side, no matter what. I would've helped you through that. We might have been young, but we weren't *that* young. I was ready to make a life with you, a family, and I would have stood by your side if you needed me. I'm just sorry that I didn't seem like a man who could do that for you."

I shook my head, leaving his hold so I could try to get my thoughts in order. "Like I said, I was young and scared and probably a little stupid, too. I'm not young and scared anymore. But I'm also not the same woman I was. We're taught at a young age that we can't be whole unless we're *truly* whole. I've learned differently. We are taught as females that we cannot truly be women without a way to bear young and be the perfect mother. And I spent countless hours trying to figure out exactly how to make that statement untrue."

"Having a uterus doesn't make you a woman, Lauren. And I know that sounds idiot coming from a man, but I don't really know what else to say other than I don't see you differently because of the hell you went through. No, that's wrong, I see you as stronger than you once were, and I already thought you were pretty damn strong."

I couldn't help but smile at his words. But I knew the expression didn't quite reach my eyes. "I know that. I know that I'm still a woman even though I had a hysterectomy far too young. I know that I'm still a woman even though I can never have a child of my own. And I know that there are many other ways to have children that have nothing to do with carrying one to term. I know all of that. The facts were laid out before me, and I can even say that with a straight face and feel the truth of it now. But I didn't feel that way when it first happened. I thought someone had torn away the part of me that made me *me*, the part of me that made me a woman in the eyes of society and those I cared about. That's what I thought when everything first happened. So I couldn't call you. I couldn't call the boy I loved and tell him that I wasn't the same girl he had fallen for. That I was a girl who could run away because she was scared. I couldn't do that. So I let time pass and thought maybe you could move on and find your happily ever after. All the while, I just tried to heal. And it wasn't just my body. It was also my mind. And like you said, I'm stronger now." I swallowed hard. "I'm stronger now." I repeated the words as if a mantra to myself. I had said them to myself over and over again over the years as an exercise, and it had helped. And yet being in front of Brandon right then, some tendrils of fear and inadequacy were slowly weaving their way through my system. I knew if I didn't get it out soon, I might break again. And I refused to do that.

"You are so strong. And I don't know what it means that you're back in town and that you happened to walk into my tattoo shop, but I have to think it happened for a reason. Don't you?"

I really, really wanted that to be the case. My hands were shaking, and my stomach hurt. I'd been doing a good job of living my life day by day, trying to be this new Lauren I'd become. But my job had brought me back to Denver, and my need for a symbol of the supposed strength I held had brought me back to Brandon. I wasn't sure I could handle them both.

"Lauren?" There was such vulnerability in his voice that I knew I would probably break whatever fragile trust we had established in the past hour we'd been in each other's presence again, but I needed to breathe.

"I'm so glad I got to tell you why I left. I'm so happy that I got to see you and get a glimpse of the man you've become. But being near you reminds me of what I lost. What *we* lost. I don't know if I can do that. It brings me back to the time when I couldn't breathe. When I couldn't stand on my own. The time my body betrayed me when I shouldn't have had to worry. I don't think I can stay, Brandon. I don't think I can be here anymore. Thank you for giving me the opportunity to tell you why I left. I hope your life is amazing. Just…without me."

And with that, his hand fell to his side, and I turned on my heel and walked out the door, leaving him behind like I had done once before. But this time, in a way I knew would probably break me in the end. I hadn't meant to see him today, hadn't known if I would ever see him again. Denver, after all, was a big place.

I hated myself for leaving, but I knew I might hate myself even more if I stayed.

I couldn't go down that road again, couldn't let those memories slam into me one by one. So I would walk away and let Brandon live his life as he had been. And, one day, maybe I might be able to find my own path. One day.

CHAPTER 4

BRANDON

I could still hear the echo of her words, the sound of her shoes against the hardwood of my floor as I stood in my living room, trying to figure out what the hell had just happened and what I was going to do about it.

So much had been thrown at me, I wasn't sure I could possibly figure it all out at once. The thing was, though, I didn't have to figure it out for myself. She left because she was scared, just like she had left before. But unlike last time, I didn't have to watch her run away. If she truly wanted me out of her life, I would let that happen. I wouldn't go all stalker on her and force myself somewhere I wasn't wanted. But she needed to know who I was now. Because I had seen the strength in her, and though she had left, saying she wasn't strong enough, I didn't think that was the case. From the look in her eye, I think she knew that, too. She was scared, and I couldn't blame her. But I couldn't just let her go. Not again. Maybe if I begged, she would stay. I wasn't too proud to beg. No matter what people thought about big, bearded, tattooed men. I would go down on my knees and plead. Because I had let her walk out of my life once before, and honestly, I didn't think I was strong enough to do it again.

I quickly ran out of my apartment, hoping I could catch her before she turned off on some block, and I lost her forever. I didn't have her number, wasn't even on social media myself beyond what I needed to show off my art for work, so I couldn't find her that way either. Plus, if I did that, that would be a little too stalkerish for me. So I would hope that she was still near enough to the building that I could still find her.

Because as she had spoken earlier, I realized that even though we had both changed, one thing remained the same. I still loved her. There was a reason I hadn't had a strong connection or any commitments with any of the men or women I had been with in the time since Lauren. There was a reason I always pushed everybody away so they didn't get too close. It was because I was waiting for her. That may sound crazy, might sound as if I were putting all of my hopes and dreams into a revenant of my past, but that wasn't the case. I'd seen my friends fall for the loves of their lives one by one over time, and I knew one thing for certain. Once you found the person—or sometimes *people* as in Maya's case—you knew was meant for you and was wrapped around your soul so tightly that you couldn't tell where one person ended and the other began, you didn't let them go. You fought. You fought for what you could have and what you wanted. You talked to each other and figured out what you needed, and what you wanted. There was no running away from the hard things. And even though I knew that Lauren had a damn good reason to fear the memories I had brought back up for her, she didn't have a clear picture of who I was now. She didn't know how we could be together now. It had been six years, and yet seeing her had brought back every single moment of passion, love, and need I remembered. I loved her even more now, and I prayed I'd be able to find her because I didn't want to lose her again.

I ran down the stairs, not bothering to take the elevator that wasn't that old but felt like it, and slammed open the outer door. The fresh Denver air mixed with the scents of the inner-city filled my nostrils, and I looked everywhere I could for those chestnut waves. And because, perhaps, fate decided to be on my side for once in my life, I didn't have to look far.

She sat on a bench right outside my apartment building. Others walked past us, unaware of the heartache and tension that lay bare between the two of us. Of course, no one really knew what truly went on between two people unless they stopped and studied them or perhaps asked. And, now, I was getting way too philosophical when I should be trying to figure out what I was going to say to her. She'd run from my apartment, from my building, but she hadn't gone far. Could I count that as a sign? A step in the right direction? Or maybe she'd known where she was going when she left. I tried not to think that the latter could be true, but knowing her—or at least knowing who she once was—I really didn't know the answer.

She hadn't noticed me yet, and for that, I was grateful. It gave me a few moments to collect my thoughts and figure out what to say. Because I was going to say something. I wasn't sure I could watch her walk away. Walk out of my life just like before. I was going to take a chance and hope she wanted me back, even with everything else going on around us. And if she said no, if she said it was too much, I would walk away. *I* would do the walking this time so she didn't have to. Because that was how much I had once loved her, and a testament to what I felt for her now. But I hoped to hell that she didn't want either of us to walk away this time.

I hadn't stopped thinking about her over the years, even though I probably should have so I could move on. But maybe there was a reason there hadn't been anybody else for me. I could have fallen for any of the men or women I was with during the time when Lauren was out of my life, yet I hadn't. I hadn't even allowed myself to get close enough to do that. Just as she had said she had walled herself off to heal and figure out who she was, I had done the same thing. I had pushed everybody away from me so no one could hurt me again. Sure, I had found friends, had grown close to those at the shop, but I never let anyone else into my soul, into my heart. That place was Lauren's. And I hoped to hell she'd let me show her that.

"You should come inside," I said after a moment, not knowing what else to say. "I promise I won't touch you, promise I won't make you make any promises you don't want, but it's a little too chilly out for you to be sitting on a bench when my place is right behind you."

She turned at the sound of my voice, her eyes wide. Thankfully, though, there were no tears running down her cheeks. I wasn't sure I could handle it if she were crying. I'd never been good with Lauren's tears. I could handle anyone else's sadness, and was actually one of the ones at the shop that was good for hugs and consoling, but I couldn't handle it when the love of my life cried. That was probably a fault in my case, considering I'd just thought of her as the love of my life. If she let me, I'd find a way to make it work. If she allowed it, I'd find a way to make everything work.

"I ran again." Lauren winced, but I didn't move

closer. There were two feet separating us, a large enough space that I couldn't feel the heat of her, but close enough that I could see every reaction on her face, every bit of the tension in her shoulders and the tight clench of her fists. "I didn't mean to run. I promised myself that I would never run again. And yet, an hour with you, and all I could do was go back to my old habits. What does that say about me that I did that so quickly?"

I frowned. "There's nothing wrong with you. I'm going to have to make sure you get that out of your head if we are going to keep talking." I did my best to put a mock-scowl on my face as I said the words, and her lips quirked up into a small smile. I would count that as a win.

"Since you sound so stern, I guess I should believe you." This time, a single tear tracked down her cheek, and I couldn't help but take a step forward and reach out to brush it off her face.

"Don't cry. I can't take it when you cry. I don't quite know what that says about me, but it's something I can work on. Come inside? Let's just talk. I promise, we can just talk."

"Will talking really help? Because what I said at the end there, what I said the whole time…that hasn't changed in the last five minutes. All that has is me sitting on this bench, wondering what to do. I hate the fact that I ran away again. That's not me anymore. Yet I went right back to my old ways without even blinking."

I sat down next to her on the bench, not liking that I was hovering over her. I was already so much bigger than she was, but I tried not to make my size an issue. She was just so tiny compared to me, fragility wrapped up in strength. I'd always thought that, and now hearing about how she had spent the past six years, I thought it even more.

"The fact that you told me everything you did and didn't break down, not even once, tells me that you didn't resort back to type—whatever that means. Because, Lauren, I fell in love with a strong woman, and you're even stronger now. I understand that having me in your life, even if it's just in passing, could bring back those bad memories, but I really hope that you can take my presence for just a bit longer so you can hear what I have to say."

She gave me a strange look and then stood up. "I guess we should go back upstairs, because I'm really not in the mood to air all of my dirty laundry to the entire city."

"Sounds like a plan." I stood up as well and took her hand. When she didn't pull back, I once again counted that as a win. If things kept going like this, before I knew it, I'd have a whole jarful of wins.

Soon, we were standing in my living room again, and

I didn't even bother to get her a glass of water. It should have felt awkward, yet just having her near me soothed any anxious nerves I might've been feeling. That alone told me that we were here for a reason, and I needed to make sure she understood that.

"I get that seeing me hurts."

She shook her head. "No, it's not that. Seeing you just reminds me of who I used to be and everything that I went through."

I frowned. "I get that, I really do. But isn't it the same as you looking in a mirror and seeing who you are now? Because every time we look at ourselves, we see the people we have become and those we were in the reflections. And I know that sounds awfully deep, but seeing you again just makes my mind go in a thousand different directions, and all those memories assault me over and over again. Yet I need that. You are the best thing that ever happened to me. Even after all these years, you are still the best thing that has ever happened to me. Maybe that's saying something about the lack of what I've had in recent years, but maybe it's saying more about what we had when we were together. I know it sounds crazy, and I never used to believe in destiny and fate of all that, but you walked into my tattoo shop for a reason. Of all the places in the world you could've gone, you walked in right in front of me. And I can't take that for granted. I have to believe that it happened for a reason. And because of that reason, I don't want you to run away again. I don't want to lose you, have you disappear from my life when I just got you back. And I'm not talking about forevers or promises or anything more, I'm talking about us in general. In this moment. I've only had you back in my life for a little over an hour, yet I don't think I could deal if you left again. I don't think I could handle it if I were the one to walk away. Because that's what I would do, Lauren. If you needed me to go because it was too much, I wouldn't force myself into your life. I would be the one to walk away this time so you didn't have to. That's how much I care for you. Before and, frankly, that love never went away. I don't know what this means, I don't know what's gonna happen in the next ten minutes let alone the next ten weeks, but I want you to take a chance on me. I don't want you to leave. Please, don't leave."

Tears flowed freely down her face now, but I didn't help her wipe them away. I did hold her hand and lowered my head, though. I rested my forehand against hers, and knew I had rambled far too much. Hopefully, she'd been able to glean at least a fragment of what I was feeling from the words.

"I just said a lot." I let out a laugh and shook my head slowly. "We can take everything I said in shifts if you want, to try and figure out exactly what I meant. But in a nutshell, I loved you then, and that feeling never went away. I just hid it really well because I missed you so damn much. But since you're back in town, I would love to get to know you again. I would love to figure out who you are and let you figure out who I am. What do you say, Lauren? Do you think you can do that?"

I stood there in silence, waiting for her to finally speak. When she opened her mouth, a laugh rang out, and warmth filled me. She wasn't laughing at me. There was too much heart in her eyes. No malice or anything else that could break both of us.

"You really know how to lay it all out there, don't you, Brandon?"

"I try. You should ask my friends. Sometimes, I just don't know when to shut up."

She smiled widely then, and the tension in my shoulders eased. "I'd like to get to know you. I want to find out who you are. And you're right, every time I look into a mirror and see myself, I know what I've been through. Looking at you doesn't bring me back to the pain, looking at you brings me back to the fact that I ran. But the thing is, I needed to run. I needed to become who I am now so I could figure out how to live this new life of mine day by day. My only regret is that I hurt you in the process."

"Never regret doing what you had to do to heal. I could say I forgive you for running away, but then I'd have to ask for your forgiveness for pushing you away at the same time. Because we both had our faults. We are both to blame for what happened back then. But now that you're back, I want to learn who you are. I want to figure out who we could be together because I missed you, Lauren. I missed you in my life. I want you to meet my friends, and I want you to stay. I don't want to run away, and I don't want you to run away either."

"So, what do we do next? Because I feel like we're going about this backwards. Because I still love you, even though that love should have faded long ago. It couldn't. It can't. But I also want to take things a little slow because I wasn't prepared for you, Brandon. Wasn't prepared six years ago, and I'm damn sure not prepared now."

"Well, that part is easy. How about we go to one of the many coffee places that happen to be on every corner of every block in the city and sit and talk? Because I want to know where you've been, what you've done, and why you're back. And I'd love to know why you walked into Montgomery Ink."

She blushed, and I couldn't help but remember exactly how she used to blush like that when we were together. Because my Lauren had blushed all over. And I'd done my best to lick up every inch of that rosy skin.

"First, stop thinking about sex, Brandon. You're making it really hard to think when you're giving me that look with those darkening eyes of yours."

I held up my hands, caught. "Sorry."

"Sure, you are. And second, I wanted a tattoo on my side with a few flowers and vines that never break. Because I didn't break, even if I wanted to."

"I'm doing your tattoo," I said quickly. "I know you probably came because of Austin or Maya since they're the famous ones in the shop, but no one else is touching your skin but me."

She raised a brow, but she didn't look angry at my outburst. "You always were possessive."

I shrugged. "Of course, I am. It's what I do." I moved forward and cupped her face again, loving the way she melted into me.

"I want you to do my tattoo, Brandon. I don't know if I could have gone through with it if I hadn't seen you at the shop. You were always my artist, you know. Always will be, no matter how many years have passed."

I didn't think anything could have made me love her more than I did in that moment. So I did the one thing I'd wanted to do since I saw her walk into Montgomery Ink.

And when she sank into me, I knew that no matter how slow we went at first, no matter how many steps we would need to take to figure out who we were now, I had found my person, my woman.

Finally.

EPILOGUE

BRANDON

Some time later….

I'd known the moment I met Lauren all those years ago that she would be important to me. I just didn't know how important. I didn't realize that it would take being apart longer than we were together for me to realize the depth of my feelings for her and the breadth of who we could be together.

We took six months to get to where we were today, and I wouldn't change any hour—any second—of any of those days. We went slowly like she asked, not touching except to kiss and learn each other's new lives. Until three months into our new relationship. Making love to Lauren would always be one of the most treasured experiences of my life.

Making love to my *wife*...well, now, that was something I would never forget until the end of my days—and perhaps even after.

Because, somehow, this woman with all of her strength and grief had agreed to become my wife. That morning, we had spoken our vows, promised our bonds to one another with her new friend Callie by her side, and Derek by mine, and now, we were husband and wife.

I never would have thought that after a long day of working on a tattoo where I had thought that one piece of art would be the sole reason for my good day could lead to this. Everything we had gone through had led to this moment, and I was still blown away by the depth of the feelings I had for this woman.

My Lauren.

My wife.

She stood in front of me, her long hair flowing around her shoulders as she tugged at her wedding dress. The guests had long since left for the evening, and now it was just the two of us in a fancy hotel room about to make love for the first time as husband and wife. I wasn't going to freak out, not really, but I was damn close to doing so.

"Why did I get a dress with so many buttons?" Lauren wiggled in her dress, trying to reach them, but it only made her breasts jiggle and almost fall out of the top.

I was pretty sure my cock would end up with zipper marks soon if I didn't get her out of that damn dress.

"That's what husbands are for," I said, my voice low and a bit rough.

"Oh, yeah? That's all you're good for?"

I growled and made my way to her in three strides, my hands sliding down the back of her dress. Keeping my eyes on hers, I undid the pearl buttons on the back, one by one.

"You're pretty good at that," she breathed. "Have a lot of practice, do you?"

My fingers fumbled with a button, and we both let out a nervous laugh. "I was doing okay without practice until you mentioned in." Unable to hold it back any longer, I kissed her, hard, and finished undoing her dress.

The silky material fell around her, and I helped her step out of it. She wore some sort of corset thing, and I went to my knees right in front of her in thanks.

"Dear God. I think I could come right here, just looking at you."

"Always the romantic," she teased, then leaned forward to kiss me.

She'd taken off her shoes already since they were pretty but she'd said they pinched her feet, and she wasn't all that much taller than me while I knelt.

I cupped her ass, bringing her closer so I could deepen the kiss. Then, somehow, we were on the large, king-sized bed with rose petals scattered beneath us. I kissed down her neck, over the generous swell of her breasts, and along her corset-covered stomach. I kissed her scars constantly, trying to show her in both actions *and* words how much I valued her—loved her. Now, she didn't shy away from me like she had the first time.

But that was behind us, as were all of our histories. Every single moment of our time together and apart had been to strengthen what we had together now. I would always remember that, even if some of those memories still hurt. I pushed those thoughts to the side for now and kept kissing her.

"I need you. I need you inside me. We can go slow after the first time, but I don't want to wait."

I swallowed hard at Lauren's words and nodded before moving up to strip out of my clothes. Together, we took off her corset and stockings, each of us wanting to be bare for our first time as man and wife. We would play with those things later, I knew, but for now, I wanted skin-to-skin, and I knew Lauren *needed* it.

I sucked and licked at her breasts, my hand between her legs as I brought her closer and closer to the edge. She was already so wet and ready, and my cock was hard enough that I knew I'd go quickly, so I didn't wait.

We'd both been tested and forgone condoms since the beginning of our new path, so it didn't take long for me to position myself at her entrance.

"I love you," I whispered, lowering my mouth to hers but not fully kissing her yet.

"Love you back." She arched up into me as I entered her, her inner walls tightening around me with each gentle thrust.

We'd made love, fucked, and had gone against walls and doors in the past, and I knew we would do all of that again soon, but for this first time as man and wife, we would go slow.

We would just *be*.

Something we hadn't been able to do before she walked into Montgomery Ink and back into my life.

Her hips rose, meeting mine thrust for thrust, and when we kissed again, we both came, our bodies far too needy to make this first time last more than a few moments. I didn't care, knowing there would be extended times in the future, but for the first time as a true *us* rather than whom we once were? I would take it.

As she ran her hands down my back, I did the same to her side, my fingers tracing over the lilies, roses, and vines I had tattooed on her. It had taken two sessions, and I'd hated seeing her hurting in any way, but in the end, her ink was the most important piece I had ever done in my entire life. I was as deep in her skin as she was in my soul.

She'd given me something special, and not just her heart.

"I'm so glad I came back." She played with the ends of my hair that I'd kept long just for her. "It's as if I never left, and yet those years are what made us who we are now."

I nodded, too choked up to speak until I cleared my throat. "Crazy to think of everything that's happened, but I'm so damn glad you're mine."

She smiled then, her face pure happiness without any hint of the shadows I'd seen six months before. "And you're mine, Brandon. Forever." She waved her hand, the light glinting off the diamond and rubies I'd put there.

"I'll take that."

And I would until the end of time. Because while I had thought I was happy before, I now knew that I'd only been at a rest stop in my life until she walked back into it —before trying to run away again.

And with another kiss to my wife's gorgeous lips, I set about showing her exactly what she'd walked into that fateful day at Montgomery Ink.

Fate and ink had given us a second chance, and no matter what lay in front of us, I wouldn't take that for granted. Ever.

INK BY NUMBERS

A MONTGOMERY INK: COLORADO SPRINGS ROMANCE

Kaylee knows art, friendship, and love. And because she's known love, she wants nothing to do with it ever again. She likes her life just the way it is. Her art and her Brushes with Lushes classes keep her sane and happy.

Landon spends his days with numbers and financial spreadsheets. At night, he just wants to relax, but the only way he can do that is with a woman. But these days, not just any woman will do.

Kaylee and Landon do an excellent job of dancing around each other, but no matter how much desire burns between them or their own personal hang-ups, they'll need to make a choice: life as they know it, or a life that could be so much more.

CHAPTER 1

*O*ne night a month, Kaylee knew she'd laugh, maybe get a little drunk, and fall in love with art all over again. It didn't matter that she was constantly surrounded by it, or that she worked with it and lived *in* it daily.

She knew she'd found her calling when she watched those who might not know art or those who thought they were horrible at it, fall for art, stroke by stroke, sip by sip.

So, yes, her monthly fun evening of Brushes With Lushes rejuvenated her, even if it might sound silly to anyone in the so-called upper crust of the art world.

And didn't *that* just make her roll her eyes?

She'd lived in that world for far too long. The elegant suits and dresses, the perfectly coiffed hair, the lifted chins and lowered eyes. She'd had all of that—the money, the style, the levels of society, and the expectations.

She'd been born into that, had been taught to thrive in it, but she had broken from it when she realized that she didn't like the Kaylee she'd become.

Kaylee had run away from that life as soon as she was able to. She was still her mother's disappointment, but that was something she was used to. Her mom hadn't wanted her to be an artist, hadn't wanted her to do something that made her happy. Honestly, Kaylee wasn't sure if her mother wanted her to be truly happy in any sense of the word.

Because happiness wasn't a family name, it wasn't becoming what or who her family was destined to be. It didn't lead to the next connection, didn't strengthen the bonds between those who made money, and those who elevated their statuses.

Happiness wasn't any of that.

And being an artist, daring to explore creativity in anything other than a hobby wasn't something Kaylee's mother could comprehend.

Kaylee had fallen in love with the idea of art, had fallen for the idea of what art could be. It might not make sense to others, but it made sense to her. She usually threw the parts of herself that didn't make sense on canvas and prayed she could find a resolution. It didn't always work. *One* person in particular in her life, someone not her mother, never came out on the canvas the right way.

But Kaylee was an artist, she was a believer, and she was free.

What she loved most about it was that she could just *be* without thinking about what her mother might want her to be. And she didn't need to think about the expectations that she had clearly given up on long ago.

Tonight, though, was not about memories, it was about *making* memories. Tonight, she would not think about her mother, she would not think about the life she'd left behind—and good riddance, thank you very much. She would not think about any of that.

She would not think about her ex-husband, she would not think about the other men that her mother had wanted her to marry after that. She would not think about the list of eligible bachelors that her mother routinely sent to her.

Mailed, not emailed. Not sent by carrier pigeon, not even by text. No, her mother painstakingly hand-wrote every single name in the most perfect cursive ever, almost calligraphy, and sent Kaylee the names of who she thought her daughter should marry next.

It was bad enough that Kaylee was a divorcee, but in her mother's eyes, she could *not* remain single at her old age.

That age only being in her thirties, but that wasn't

something she was going to talk about. She wasn't vain, but she did not like talking about her age. It wasn't as if she were old, but her mother made her feel that way every time she sent along a new skin cream for Kaylee to try. A fancy night cream to help with those wrinkles. Wrinkles she wasn't sure existed yet, but they were waiting, lurking under the surface for her to stop paying attention.

But she would wear them as a badge because it told her that she lived...even while they told her mother that she was old and dying and still childless and unwed.

And, here she was, thinking about everything that she'd told herself she wouldn't think about.

Tonight was about art. She wasn't going to be making her own art per se, but she *was* going to be watching her friends and those who came in using a coupon or just walked in for the experience of making art. This was one of her favorite nights of the month. This is when Brushes With Lushes truly came to life.

She hadn't been the first person to come up with the idea of drinking a little wine while hanging out with your friends and painting a picture. It hadn't been her original idea to stand up in front of a crowd and show them exactly how to do it, almost as if it were Paint by Numbers but not quite. Because every single canvas ended up individual in the end. Every single painting was unique to the artist. Every moonscape was somewhat different, every tree angled slightly differently. And *that* was what she loved. Because even those who claimed they didn't have a shred of artistic ability in their bones still ended up with art at their fingertips.

Art is what she craved, and that is what made her evening.

Because while she could expunge every single ounce of who she was and throw it on a canvas, sometimes, she just needed to breathe. Sometimes, she just needed to experience the energy that came from those who also wanted to show their art, or those who were too afraid to pick up a brush before. Showing others that they could be creative was what made *her* creative. At least, in a sense.

So, maybe she sometimes felt like an emotional vampire by doing these things, but she truly loved doing it. All over the country—and even in the world now that she thought about it since her friend had started one in Paris—people were holding events like this. And she loved it.

As she walked out into the main area of her studio that she had redesigned into a Brushes With Lushes storefront, she smiled. People walked in and out of the rows and around the easels, talking with each other and pouring wine. Kaylee's two assistants helped with that, making sure that everybody was happy—but not *too* happy if they were the ones with the car keys.

There would be no drinking and driving when it came to those who created in her store. Because while she would allow them to expel some of their emotions onto a canvas—even if her mother would say it was merely a moonscape—there was no way she was going to allow any of them to get into a car and possibly end up hurting themselves or someone else because of stupid decisions.

So, most people had a designated driver in their group, or they used a car service. In the age of the apps where with just two little presses of a finger, a car would come to you, there was no need to indulge and then get behind the wheel.

At least, that's what Kaylee hoped.

"I can't wait for tonight," Roxie said with a grin. Roxie Marshall, formerly Roxie Montgomery-Marshall smiled up at her, and Kaylee couldn't help but smile right back. Roxie was gorgeous, just like the rest of the Montgomerys. She had long, dark hair, but hers was a little lighter than the rest of her siblings. Her wide, blue eyes glinted with a bit of wickedness and a whole lot of happiness, something that Kaylee had not seen in her friend's eyes for far too long.

But now Roxie was happily married, she and her husband making it through their rough patch.

And the woman actually looked excited to paint. A far cry from her trepidation of the past.

Kaylee tapped her chin. "You know, I don't think I've ever actually heard you say that and mean it while in my studio."

Kaylee leaned over and hugged Roxie close, kissing her friend on the temple. In some respects, Kaylee was still new when it came to hanging out with this group of friends. She had met them because of Brushes With Lushes, and though she had met lots of women and men in her studio, it was the Montgomerys and their close-knit group that she had been drawn to.

And now she was one of them, and she loved it.

"I've been happy when I walk through these doors. I promise you."

"You say that, but you never looked very excited to paint. Aren't you the one who always says you can never get it just right?"

Roxie blushed and shook her head. "Yes, I'm a little anal when it comes to making sure I get the brushstrokes right. But Carter is making sure to tell me every chance he gets that I'm perfect just the way I am. And that I don't have to constantly compare myself to my siblings. Which isn't easy, but I'm doing better."

"And you have no idea how happy that makes me. Because I've always told you that you can do anything you want to, that you can be anybody you want to be inside this studio. The paintbrush is just the tool to show you who you are, and I know that you're an artist. You don't have to be the same kind of artist as your sisters or your sister-in-law or even your best friend. You can be your own artist."

"And I think I'm finally listening. I'm sorry that I didn't before."

Kaylee just shook her head and then hugged Roxie again as the other Montgomerys and their friend Abby walked through the doors.

"I'm just glad you're here. And I'm glad that that smile is in your eyes. I think I've missed it. No, I *know* I've missed it."

Roxie blinked away tears and just kept smiling. "You're going to make me cry, and I have mascara on that I'm not 100% sure is waterproof because it's a new one that Abby let me try."

"You're wearing that mascara? No, it's not tear-proof. Sorry. But it does make your lashes look beautiful. Just don't cry." Abby bounced in and hugged them both, and Thea, Adrienne, and Shea came up, as well.

Kaylee was now a part of this large group of women. She wasn't on the outside looking in anymore, she wasn't alone, waiting to find friends.

She had them.

And her mother would hate them.

And though that might be a plus for Kaylee, it wasn't what she'd been searching for when she found her friends. It was just an added benefit.

"So, what are we painting today?" Adrienne asked, putting her coat on the rack next to their row.

"Today, we're going with another treescape, although this one will have a few more branches for you to play with."

Adrienne was a tattoo artist—one of the most talented ones in the United States if you asked Kaylee. Adrienne's cousins and her brother were also up there in the rankings, but Adrienne had a special place in Kaylee's heart. The woman had done the long row of flowers of all different kinds, climbing a trellis on Kaylee's side and hip. It wasn't completely finished yet because both of them were artists, and their ideas sometimes clashed when it came to exactly what Kaylee wanted to put on her skin. Kaylee had done the initial drawing because she couldn't help herself, but Adrienne had been the one to make it come alive.

It was a melding of both of their talents, both of their minds. And it was exactly what Kaylee wanted.

Only one other person had seen it, and though she tried not to think about that, he had loved the design, as well.

But she wasn't going to think about him. She wasn't going to think about anything like that right now. Because tonight was about art. It was about friendship and wine.

Everything was better with wine.

"We need to get started. But, Adrienne, you're going to come by later this week, right? I know that you wanted to try that new canvas I bought."

"Oh, yes, I'm thinking oils this time. I've done water-colors and acrylics, but I've never worked with oils."

"I think you might like them. I know it's completely different than what you do with your tattoos, but maybe this outlet will help you push your art in a new direction and enhance what you already love doing."

"I love when you guys talk art, it makes me so happy. Because sometimes I feel like I have no idea what I'm doing," Thea said, setting her stuff down next to her chair.

"I've seen the way you decorate cakes," Kaylee said, leaning against the table. She did her best not to put all of her weight on it because she knew it might topple over if she did. She had strong tables, but the last thing she needed was all the easels and wine falling to the floor. Not that she had done that before or anything.

Thea shrugged. "Yes, I play with frosting. But it's not really the same as working with oils or anything like that."

"I don't know what it is with all you guys thinking that what you do isn't amazing and worthwhile. You need to stop comparing yourselves to each other and just love what you do."

"We're working on it," Abby said, her voice a little

soft. Abby was the gentlest of them. She had been through hell and back, had lost everything she loved, save her daughter, but now she was in a new relationship with one of Kaylee's good friends. Abby and Ryan were adorable together and were steadily moving into something far more serious than just dating. Kaylee had a feeling that there would be wedding bells soon, and not just for the Montgomerys.

So many weddings, so many loves, so much emotion in such a short time.

But Kaylee was just fine being alone.

She wasn't going to think about that man. Wouldn't think about his face as it flashed in her mind. She wasn't going to think about Landon.

Damnit, she'd thought his name.

No, she wasn't going to think about it.

Shea came up and kissed Kaylee on the temple. "Do you want to talk about what's on your mind?" the other woman asked.

Shea was married to the Montgomery girls' brother, Shep. They had moved from New Orleans and were now raising their little girl up in Colorado Springs. Shea was an accountant just like Roxie, and Shep owned the tattoo shop with Adrienne. It was all one big, happy family. But Shea sometimes saw far too much.

"I'm fine. But we're running a little late, so I should get started."

Kaylee quickly went up to the front of the room before anybody could question her further. She didn't like being on that end. She liked to stand in front of her friends and make sure they were fine. She enjoyed being the one dissecting things and ensuring that they were emotionally ready for the next step, that they weren't hiding from themselves. She didn't think of herself as a therapist or psychiatrist, but she did know that art helped heal. She knew that it helped bring out emotions you thought were hidden, ones that maybe didn't need to be behind so many layers.

Kaylee put herself into everything she did, including her work. And tonight would be no different.

But that didn't mean she liked being on the other side of that lens.

"Okay, ladies and gentlemen," she said as the women in the room laughed. The lone male just shook his head and raised his glass of pinot noir.

"Okay, I guess gentle*man*, welcome to Brushes With Lushes. Tonight, we're going to have a little fun, and maybe a whole lot more. I do hope that you put whatever you want into your paintings tonight. You don't have to do what I do. Just use my steps as a basis for what you'd like to do. Indulge in what you like. Know that no one here is going to judge. Because if they do, I know exactly how to kick them on their rear and get them out of here."

She paused as the class laughed, just as she intended them to.

"Okay, then, let's start with a blank canvas. Some say it's the scariest part of all, but I think of it as a beginning. It's just begging for paint, just as a blank page begs for words. And, so, we shall indulge."

The evening went off without a hitch, and the paintings that came out of it made her grin. Everybody had started with what she had given them and made it his or her own. That was what she loved. She wanted to see who they were through what they put on the canvas. Some of them were a little darker, some a little more comical. Some were romantic and light, others a little more nightmarish.

It was exactly what she needed.

THE CLASS FILTERED OUT, AND KAYLEE HUGGED AND kissed her friends as they walked away, all of them having their own lives to go back to. She let her assistants leave as soon as the place was cleaned up. Soon, she was alone —exactly what she was used to.

Maybe that helped her art, but she didn't know.

She let out a breath and closed her eyes, knowing she had a long night of art ahead of her. Her fingertips had been burning with the idea of what came to mind while she was helping others. She didn't have a project in the works at the moment. Everything was in one stage or another, but she hadn't started anything new in about a month. Maybe that should've worried her, but that was how she worked. She threw herself into multiple things at once and took breaks.

But, tonight...tonight, she would start something new.

As she opened her eyes, she knew she wasn't alone anymore. *He* was there.

He wasn't just on her mind, he was right behind her.

So she rolled her shoulders back and turned, making sure to keep her gaze cool.

"You're late," she said, her voice low. "The evening's already over."

The man shook his head and brushed his knuckle across her jaw. She didn't flinch, didn't back away, but she didn't lean in to him either. Because she couldn't. She couldn't do anything but look at him. "I'm not late. I can't be. Not when it comes to you."

"That doesn't even make sense."

He let out a chuckle. "I was trying to be romantic."

"There's no need to be romantic, Landon. You're not mine. Remember? We tried that once, and it didn't work out."

That had been the last time she was with *any* man. Kaylee tried not to wince at the idea of her dry spell, but she and Landon were not a couple. They had tried, and it hadn't worked. All of their friends wanted to know more, but that just meant she wasn't going to tell them. She didn't know why it hurt that it hadn't worked out between them. She wasn't sure what she wanted, and he didn't want a relationship. It just didn't work.

And if she kept telling herself that, maybe it wouldn't hurt so much anymore.

"I just missed you."

She closed her eyes, letting out a breath. "You can't say things like that, Landon. And I need to go to work. Was there something you wanted?"

He just looked in her eyes and then slowly shook his head. "I just wanted to make sure you were okay. I was driving by and saw the lights on but no cars in the parking lot. You know it worries me when you're here all alone."

"I'm alone a lot of the time, Landon. I'm used to it."

"You should have someone taking care of you, Kaylee."

"I can take care of myself. You're not the one who's going to be taking care of me. Remember?"

"Will you be in your studio all night?"

She let out a breath. "Yes, and your desk is all set for you if you'd like to sit and do your work and watch me."

He just smiled. The two of them walked back to her studio, closing up the rest of the front of the shop. They went to work—him doing paperwork and working with spreadsheets that made her eyes cross, and her ignoring him to the best of her ability as she threw everything she had at the canvas.

He didn't like her to be alone, knew that she really didn't like it even though she told herself she was fine with it.

Because he liked to take care of her, even if she wasn't his to take care of.

Their relationship was complicated, but so many other things were, as well. They were friends, had been lovers, but they were never anything more than that.

And just because some part of her wanted that, didn't mean it would ever happen.

Because it couldn't.

And it wouldn't.

CHAPTER 2

*L*andon had been at this one spreadsheet for what felt like a week. As he looked down at the calendar on his computer, he frowned. It actually *had* been a week. Seven days since he'd gotten this account, and it was getting a little ridiculous that he was still working on it and trying to make the numbers work. Well, maybe not work but at least make sense. He loved his job. He enjoyed making sure others made money, and he really loved the fact that *he* could make money. What he didn't like was when his clients wanted to make money and not have to spend it. They just wanted it to happen overnight, and apparently, it was Landon's job to make that happen.

Even in his line of work, he was not a risk-taker. He couldn't be. He couldn't afford it. Yes, others could be doing his job—he was a broker, after all. He was also a financial planner for some. That used to be his main job, and he was thinking about going back to it. He wasn't sure he liked what he was doing any longer, but maybe that was because he was restless about so many other things.

No, he wasn't going to think about that. He really wasn't going to think about what he was restless about. He wasn't going to think about anything like that. He was just going to focus on finishing up this spreadsheet and then have a beer.

A very good brew. Maybe two. Maybe even five. Okay, he wasn't in his twenties anymore, so not five.

God, when had he gotten old? Not that he actually *was* old, but sometimes, he sure felt like it. Sitting hunched over his desk, staring at numbers until his eyes crossed, was one of those times.

So, he shut down his computer after saving everything, and knew it was time for his weekend to start. He would just have to get back to it on Monday. He was good at what he did, fast at it, but sometimes, the numbers just didn't work. When they didn't, he knew it was time to back away.

Perhaps it *was* time to find a new job. One that didn't stress him out to the point where he was afraid that his hair would start falling out.

He ran a hand through his chestnut brown hair and winced.

Was it thinning? Was he getting a bald spot? His boss had a bald spot, one that seemed to grow with every passing financial cycle. Maybe that was his next stage. Balding. And a little more beer so he'd get a little rounder in the stomach. Not that he'd judge anyone for that, but he really wasn't ready for that yet.

The idea he was balding could just be related to age. Or it could be that he was doing his best not to think about the fact that one of his best friends had started to push him away.

Maybe it was because she needed to push him away.

He let out a groan and let his head fall back so he could close his eyes. He was losing his damn mind, and he was pretty sure it was all Kaylee's fault.

And if it was her fault, then it was really his fault. Because he was the asshole. He was always the asshole.

He might have let his friend stay at his house when Carter and his wife were dealing with marital problems and trying to actually communicate with each other. He might have also helped Ryan figure out what he needed to say and do when it came to the love of his life, Abby. And he was there when Dimitri and Mace needed him, when they were figuring out their love lives.

But all of that did not make him not an asshole. If he

added enough double negatives, maybe he could actually come up with something positive.

Or maybe, once again, he was letting numbers and words get into his head, and it was making him lose his freaking mind.

So, he closed up and got into his car. His nice, fancy, fully-loaded Audi with its leather interior and its new car smell. He swore he'd have to just get a new car when that smell faded.

This purchase wasn't very good with the whole financial planning thing, but it was his baby. He did not have a lot of vices. He drank light beer when he felt like it, and cheap brands most of the time when he was out with his friends. He had nice suits, but he didn't own a thousand of them. He owned a few and switched out the shirts and ties that went with them. He was good, financially responsible. And as he ran his hands over the leather of the steering wheel, he realized that he was when it came to this baby, too.

He loved this car. Loved it more than anything else in his life.

That thought made him wince.

Really? *Really, Landon? Your car is your baby? The one thing you love?*

No wonder Kaylee was getting tired of him. No wonder he was the lone male of his friends without a woman.

Yes, everybody thought that he and Kaylee were actually together, but they didn't realize that he and Kaylee had tried that once and were now just friends.

Just. Friends.

He didn't know why that hurt. It wasn't as if they hadn't tried before. It just didn't work out. She hadn't wanted a serious relationship at the time, and he didn't know if that had really changed. He loved women. He loved the way they felt, the way they laughed. He loved the way he made them feel, and the way they made *him* feel. He loved their curves, loved when they didn't have curves. He loved every part of them, and not just the way they looked.

He was not ready to settle down—or at least he hadn't been. He and Kaylee had both known the score when they fell into bed together and realized that they weren't the ones for each other. So, they had fallen right back out of bed but not out of each other's lives. They'd remained friends, and he didn't know why, but he had assumed a sort of protective role when it came to her. Protective when he knew that she didn't want it. It wasn't that she actually needed someone in that position. She was damn strong all on her own, she didn't need a man in her life. Now that he thought about it, she told him that frequently.

He didn't like her alone in her studio, and he knew that she didn't enjoy eating out alone—he wasn't really a fan of it either. So, when he didn't have a date, which was more often than not these days now that he thought about it, they went out together.

They liked trying out new restaurants, enjoyed a lot of the same food. They liked getting dressed up and feeling *fancy*. Not that he actually said that, but Kaylee had once, and now it stuck in his head.

They just liked doing a lot of the same things. So, they did. Together. It made things a little awkward sometimes because they had seen each other naked. He had licked every inch of her. They had fallen into bed way too fast, way too hard, but it had been damn good. The sex had been amazing. And everything after had been pretty amazing, as well. It was just that neither of them wanted to ruin what they had by trying for something more serious. Because they hadn't wanted anything serious.

He let out a breath and told himself that everything was fine. This weird feeling in his stomach was just because he was worried about his job and the fact that he was considering changing careers slightly. It was just because everyone around him was getting married and having babies or more babies. That's all it was. He wasn't thinking about the fact that he sort of missed his best friend in a way that wasn't so…friendly.

The Bluetooth on his car rang, and the screen popped up with Kaylee's name.

"Speak of the devil," he whispered and then winced.

Kaylee was no devil. A siren, sure. A minx, perhaps. But there was a reason the sailors went to those sirens. There was a reason their calls wooed the men and lured them closer.

If Kaylee was a siren, then he was the easily and willingly lured pirate.

Great, now he was thinking about himself in the Dread Pirate Roberts getup and she as Princess Buttercup—but in a more daring outfit.

He was officially losing his damn mind. He quickly pressed the button on his steering wheel and answered. "So, you just can't take any time without me. Can you? You miss me desperately." He over-exaggerated the words, and he could practically hear her rolling her eyes.

"You're an idiot, Landon."

"Yes, yes, I am. But only an idiot for you." He really needed to stop teasing her, but they both did that. It was just how they worked. Though he didn't know why it was starting to hurt. With every tease, every flirtation, it started to needle just a little bit. Maybe he needed to stop. Perhaps he needed to back away.

But he didn't know if he could do that.

"It's a Friday night, Landon. And I'm hungry."

He swallowed hard and used his free hand to adjust himself in his pants. As soon as she'd said those words, his mind hadn't gone to food. It went to her on her knees in front of him, hungry for something more than just a taste.

He really needed to get laid. And Kaylee was not the answer to his problem.

"Oh?"

"Stop thinking about sex, Landon."

She snapped the words, and he let out a laugh. "You're starting to freak me out with this whole mind-reading thing."

"Well, I am amazing like that. But I really want to go to that sushi place we both like. I can call in a reservation since I know it's a Friday night, but they can usually slide us in."

He was not going to think about sliding anything in.

Oh, God, he was losing his mind. Losing his fucking mind.

"I could do sushi."

"That's what I thought. Pick me up? I'll make the reservation for forty-five minutes from now. That'll give us enough time."

"Enough time for what?" he asked, his voice as low and seductive as he could possibly make it."

"Enough time to make sure you don't look as ragged as you normally do after a long day of numbers. Don't tempt me, Landon. You're not going to like the outcome."

He laughed and then hung up as she said her goodbyes.

They were both playing with fire, and he knew it. One day soon, they would land in bed together again, and he was afraid once they rolled out of it, they wouldn't be the same people anymore. He'd changed after sleeping with her the first time, and he damn well knew it would be worse this time.

Things were already messy, and it was just getting worse. He was standing in quicksand, trying to run, but there was no escape.

There never was.

"I DON'T UNDERSTAND WHY YOU LIKE THE SPICY, CRUNCHY stuff," Kaylee said, wrinkling her nose as he ate an entire spicy salmon crunchy roll. He just grinned, knowing that he was showing some of the food in his mouth.

They were at a decently upscale restaurant, and this was not how you were supposed to act, but he loved making her wince, liked making her laugh.

"You're disgusting. But I kind of knew that going in. It's sort of who you are." He swallowed after chewing and drank a gulp of water until he didn't have any more of that spiciness on his tongue.

"Oh, shush. You chew with your mouth open, too, sometimes."

"I did once, and I had a cold. A very bad one where I

couldn't breathe through my nose. I don't know why you keep bringing that up."

"Because you keep bringing up the spicy, crunchy thing." He took another bite, this one a little bit smaller so he didn't have to shove it all into his mouth. "I just like the way it tastes."

"It does taste good, but I don't like the texture of it. And I love sushi, you know that, but even some fish eggs kind of freak me out. It's the texture in your mouth. I just can't do it."

He just shook his head, took the roe that she had scraped off the top of one of the rolls, and put it on his plate.

"I can't believe you would waste this precious, precious roe."

"I'm not wasting it. I wouldn't have ordered it if you didn't like it. Because I know none of it will go to waste since you will eat it. If I were by myself—which I rarely am these days for some reason because I think everybody likes to take me out to eat—I wouldn't have ordered it at all. I would have just had Sushi Me or something. No eggs or crunchiness or anything that would feel weird in my mouth."

"Okay, back up, why did you sound sad when you said people were going out to dinner with you? Is this like a pity thing tonight?"

She shook her head. "I'm not talking about you. It's

the damn Montgomerys." She sounded so exasperated that he snorted.

"They're after you to make sure you're happy and in love just like they are, aren't they?"

She tilted her wineglass at him, raising her brow. "I see I'm not alone in the Montgomery ways."

"They just want us to be happy."

"But I hope they realize that it's not going to be with each other. Right?" She said the words very, very carefully, and he nodded just as cautiously. They did their best not to talk about this, but it had come up at least twice during the past week. Ever since he'd sat and watched her work in the studio, they had been very, very careful with each other. But then again, they were always super careful.

"They'll figure it out."

"I hope they do. And soon. Because if they don't, they're going to start forcing me to go on blind dates. That is something I do not want to do. I met my ex on a blind date."

He tilted his head, doing his best not to let his fingers clench on his chopsticks. He did not like thinking about her ex. He knew Kaylee didn't either, but the subject made Landon rage. He had never met the man, didn't even know what he was really like. But he didn't like the way her eyes changed when she talked about him. Didn't like how she sounded angry and hurt all at the same time.

So, no, he did not like her ex.

"I didn't know you met him on a blind date."

"My mother set it up."

That was all she needed to say. Landon knew all about her mother, knew about her upbringing. They had gotten drunk one night with some really expensive wine that one should not get drunk on, and they had raged about their pasts and families.

He didn't talk to his parents much, nor with his brother and his two sisters. His parents just didn't understand him.

They were good, hard-working, blue-collar people that worked two jobs just to put food on the table. They also spent way more money than they made because they thought it was their right. He didn't understand them, but that was just how they lived. They didn't get that debt was crippling, and they always thought that Landon could help them out. He had at first, but not anymore.

His brother and sisters were the same way. They didn't go to college, not because they didn't have the grades, but because they figured they didn't need it. They worked, but sometimes not as hard as their parents, and most of the time, not as hard as they should.

Their spouses and their kids just kept spending money, just as Landon's parents did.

Maybe that's why he worked with money. Because he liked to make sure that he knew what he was spending, knew what he had. And how to make more. Because he didn't want to go hungry, didn't want the debt collectors coming again. Didn't want any of that.

He blinked as Kaylee reached out and put her hand on his.

"I didn't mean to make you think about your family. We can talk about something else. Like, maybe a sports game? I'm sorry the Broncos aren't going to be in the Super Bowl."

He snorted, shaking his head. "The Super Bowl was last month. And the Broncos haven't been in the Super Bowl in a long time. And it scares me sometimes that you can read my mind like you do when it comes to my family."

She just shrugged, moving her hand back. Landon didn't know why he missed the touch. Kaylee wasn't his. And he had to remember that. They were just friends.

"I can read you because I feel the same way about mine. Now, is there another sporting event we can talk about?"

"If you call it a *sporting event* with that upper-crust, British accent that you totally don't have, we're not going to talk about it at all. We can talk about art. Maybe the newest Monet?"

"There isn't a newest Monet. There's just a Monet."

"Oh, well, it seems I'm not as cultured as I want to be."

"Oh, shush. You know your arts. You're just as fancy

as I am, you just try to hide it. Except with that car of yours. There's no hiding that."

"So, you like my car, do you?"

"You know I do. You just won't let me drive it."

"Nobody drives my baby girl."

"Men and their cars."

"And that's a fact."

Then they were both laughing, talking about nothing and everything at the same time. They split the check because neither of them liked being indebted to the other. Then he drove her home, walking in to make sure that she was safe before he left. He didn't know why he did that, but he had started it as soon as their friend, Adrienne, was attacked at the tattoo shop. Yes, maybe he was overprotective, but he didn't like the fact that Kaylee was alone. Didn't like that as soon as he left, she'd lock the door behind him, and no one would be there to help her. She might be self-sufficient, but he was still a caveman in some respects.

"Thanks for taking me to dinner," she said as she removed her coat. Landon swallowed hard as he looked at her shoulders, at her curves. Kaylee was a damn gorgeous woman. Sometimes, it was hard to remember that she wasn't his.

"You paid for half, so I guess thank you for dinner, as well."

"Well, what are you doing tomorrow night? I mean, I

have to work in the studio all day, but it's a Saturday for you. Do you have any plans with the men?"

He shook his head. "Everyone has dates with their own women. So, I guess it's just you and me tomorrow night. We can try that new Fusion place. Although, I think there was something about lentils and black seaweed and sriracha with a dash of cayenne? I really don't know about that menu."

She snorted and then sidled up to him, putting her arm around his waist. "Yeah, maybe not that place. But I can think of something. Thank you for coming out with me tonight. I didn't really want to eat at home alone. You know?"

"I know. Though you know, you could have had a date with anybody you wanted. You're fucking gorgeous, Kaylee."

She turned in his hold, and he wrapped his arms around her. She looked back at him. "You sometimes surprise me with your flattery."

He frowned. "I shouldn't. You know that I think you're beautiful, brilliant. Fucking creative. You know all of that."

"So you tell me. But you sometimes just tell me out of the blue, and it just surprises me."

"Well, then I guess I like that kind of surprise." Then he did something stupid. *So* stupid. He lowered his head and brushed his lips along hers. She gasped for a second, and he didn't think again. He just leaned in more, sliding his tongue along hers. A simple caress, an ache between them. He kissed her, softly, sweetly...and then a little harder.

Then he remembered who was in his arms. Recalled that Kaylee wasn't his. That they had already gone down this path and knew that they weren't meant for each other.

He stopped the kiss and rested his forehead on hers.

"Goodnight, Kaylee."

"Goodnight." A pause. A deep breath. "Drive safe, Landon."

He kissed her forehead in a way a friend would, how a brother would with his sister, not in a way a man would when he knew he was falling in love with the woman in his arms.

His breath caught as he walked away, that thought echoing in his head.

He couldn't love this woman. He could not be falling in love with Kaylee.

Because that's not what they were to each other.

The word scared him more than it should.

So, it wasn't true. It was just a stray thought. A lie.

He got into his car, his baby, and knew that there was a lie involved, but it wasn't that.

CHAPTER 3

$\mathcal{T}$he Stones blared out of the speakers in her studio. Kaylee threw up her hands, ignoring the paint that sprayed across the covered floor and flew into her hair as she shook her hips to the sound of Mick Jagger's voice. She swayed, shimmied, and went to her tiptoes as she sang along, letting the music and the feeling spread through her before she stood in front of the canvas and began to paint.

Yes, sometimes, she was a really messy painter. Other times, she was precise, fluid, and didn't spill a single drop.

Tonight, was not one of those times.

Tonight, she was frustrated. Not just with the day, and not just with her thoughts, but sexually.

And she was tired of being sexually frustrated.

She knew exactly whose fault it was. Oh, it wasn't

hers. It couldn't possibly be hers and her horrible, no-good, very bad thoughts about the man that she shouldn't be thinking of.

No, it all rested on *his* shoulders. Those very broad, very strong shoulders.

No, she was not going to think about that.

Or the fact that she was slowly drawing a very angry and yet sensually abstract art piece that just made her wonder what the hell she was doing.

She didn't even think as she put brush to paint and paint to canvas. She painted, she felt, and she knew that this would be an angry yet sexual piece.

And it was all Landon's fault. Landon and his very broad shoulders and his very chiseled chest, and those hips that were slender but enough to dig her fingers into. Oh, Landon and his nice ass and his thick thighs and that very nice cock.

No, she was not going to think about Landon's dick.

That was the reason she was in this situation.

She paused, laughing.

She had reached a whole new level of what the fuck was wrong with her.

Because there was something definitely wrong with her if she was singing an ode and painting a piece all about Landon's...well, piece.

She was losing her mind, and it was all his fault.

And, yes, maybe it was her fault, too. But she couldn't help it.

She was sexually frustrated, and really just needed an orgasm.

Or maybe she just needed to paint, get angry, and dance around to the Rolling Stones and whatever else came up on her playlist. She had an eclectic mix of The Stones, Guns 'n' Roses, and even some Backstreet Boys.

Because, sometimes, she didn't want it that way, and the boy bands of her youth had kept her going, even with some of the grunge and heavy metal and rock and oldies she mixed in. She loved all music, and she didn't care that boy bands were a thing for teenage girls. Because those teenage girls grew up, and they bought more tickets to the shows as the boy bands came up.

Yes, she was going to see the Backstreet Boys at their upcoming concert. She was a little too young to like the New Kids on the Block as much as some of her friends were, but she was taking the Montgomerys and Abby to see the Backstreet Boys. Each of them liked a different member, and that was very helpful. Because no one was going to touch her Brian. Her perfect, artistic soul.

She stared at her canvas, then set down the paintbrush and started laughing hysterically.

Somehow, her sexual rage had turned into a frothy piece of Brian from the Backstreet Boys.

Her art back when she was thinking about him was

much different. And it was *still* different because he had grown up, and so had she.

But Brian was no Landon.

And if Landon knew her at all, he would know that was a compliment. Not that she would actually say that to him, because there were some things you did not talk about with your friends, specifically ones you had seen naked. Especially a friend that you still wanted to see naked. No, you did not talk about your boy band crushes.

Again.

At least not without a lot of wine.

Oh, God, she'd forgotten that she already told Landon about her crush on Brian.

He had said that he liked Lance more, and then she had to explain the difference between the Backstreet Boys and N'Sync—it had been a whole thing.

"Okay, that's enough of that." She shook her head, wiped off her hands on the towel she set next to the easel, and went to change from one station to another. Maybe a playlist wasn't what she needed. Maybe she just needed random music to fill her mind.

Or, maybe she needed something to keep her from thinking about Landon.

Because she missed him. It had only been a few days since she saw him last, and yet she missed him.

She wasn't supposed to miss someone who wasn't her significant other. Yes, they were friends, but it couldn't be anything more than that. Like she'd told herself numerous times before, they had already tried that. It hadn't worked. So, why did she feel like she was losing a piece of herself when she didn't see him. He hadn't stopped by the studio, hadn't watched her work while he worked himself. It wasn't like he did that every day. Far from it. They each had their own lives, and it wasn't like they were constantly in each other's pockets. But he hadn't contacted her since sushi. Since that kiss.

But she hadn't contacted him either. She hadn't texted him, hadn't called him. Hadn't just stopped by, wondering what they were missing by not actually touching each other.

Maybe if she wasn't so in her head, if she weren't so worried about getting hurt again, she'd actually pay attention and make this into something she wanted.

But something had come over his eyes after he kissed her, something that scared her. And then he'd walked out.

And they hadn't talked since.

The rage came back again, the angry sexual tension that she knew would return to her art. So, she pulled out her paint and went back to it. She could get rid of some of the fluff that had come from Brian and the Backstreet Boys on the mind. She could focus on what she was truly feeling.

That anger, that rage, that...what-the-hell-am-I-doing when it came to her friend.

Everyone else was falling around her, they were all finding their happily ever afters. Some had taken longer to get there, and some had even fallen and had to find a way back up again. People had been hurt, some had split up, but everybody had found their happiness in the end.

She had thought she'd found her happiness before.

But it hadn't worked.

Nothing worked when it came to her it seemed.

No. Her job was good, her art was good. Everything was good.

Just because she couldn't find that *thing*, didn't mean she wasn't good.

So she let out a breath and sank into her art.

The colors flowed, and she did, too. She threw it all out onto the canvas, into her project. She let everything that she'd been thinking just fly from her fingertips and through the paintbrush. If she could throw herself into her art, just smack herself into the paper and canvas, mix with the paints, maybe it would help her. She felt like she was ripping her soul apart piece by piece, digging into the art in front of her, trying to mold it into something that made sense.

But nothing about her made sense in her mind. And maybe that was right. Maybe that's what made her art, hers.

As she tried to catch her breath, her chest moving up and down in pants, and as paint dripped from her fingers and from the brush, she knew she had done something pivotal.

This was for her. This *was* her.

Even with the blemishes of her earlier errant thoughts, even with the things that didn't make any sense, the art in front of her was Kaylee.

And for some reason, she didn't like it.

She didn't like the bold colors, and the angles and swirls made no sense. She didn't like the way the contrasting shades butted up against one another, sometimes in such a vivid expression that it startled her.

This was Kaylee.

This was fear.

This was her not being able to take that next step, not being able to communicate because she was so afraid of what was within.

This was her remembering that she had lost before— lost part of herself when she tried to fall in love with the right man. The one her mother had chosen for her. The guy she'd thought would bring her closer to her family and to who and what she should be.

Because she married that man, and no one could look down on her for not doing something she was supposed to do. Maybe she wasn't supposed to be in that society, but she could at least be with that man, could make that decision.

And then she walked away from it, making mistake after mistake and turning into the woman she was now.

Maybe it didn't make any sense, or...maybe it did.

Maybe she was putting too much meaning behind a piece of art that was just a painting.

She was an artist, and she knew that, sometimes, a painting was just a painting. It wasn't a representation of what she was or what she could be. Before she could catch her breath, before she could figure out exactly what she was going to do with the project in front of her, her phone buzzed on the table where Landon worked sometimes. She quickly wiped her hands and walked over to the phone, trailing her fingers along the desk where he usually sat. She loved when he worked there, loved when he was just there. His presence soothed her, even as it revved her up.

But they were friends. Maybe that's what friends did.

She didn't bother looking at the readout, knowing she had let the phone ring for far too long already.

But when she answered it, she knew she had made a mistake.

"Kaylee Chambers. You know better than to make me wait. What were you doing? What took you so long to answer your phone."

Kaylee closed her eyes, trying not to grind her teeth at the sound of her mother's voice. She already had dental bills to deal with from grinding her molars because of her mother. She did not want to wear a night guard like they'd suggested.

But Angelica Chambers did not know when to back down. In fact, there was no backing down when it came to her dearest daughter.

Ever.

"Hello, Mother. I'm sorry it took me so long to get to the phone. But I'm here now. What can I do for you?" She made her voice sound as pleasant as possible. She had long since given up trying to be herself or even sarcastic with her mother. It never led to anything good and always made the conversation last longer. The more she made herself accommodating, at least for certain periods of time, the quicker the conversation would be over, and the less time she had to deal with her mother or her mother's problems.

"Don't get that tone with me."

"What can I do for you, Mother?" Kaylee asked again, keeping her voice pleasant. There was no tone, but her mother always heard it no matter what Kaylee said. Because that was her mother. Dearest Angelica, the one who didn't make mistakes but who had a daughter who *was* a mistake.

"I'm calling because your trust is waiting, yet you're not doing anything to deserve it."

"You don't deserve a trust, Mother. It comes when you're born because someone signs it over to you."

"That is enough, Kaylee."

"If that's all, I'm going to go now. I'm working."

"Art. Or whatever you call it. We Chambers do not work with our hands, Kaylee. Your grandfather set up that trust for you, and your father made sure it was just right for you for when you got married and had children. You need to live the life a respectable Chambers should. I do not understand why you don't understand this. You keep walking away from your family, from your responsibilities. And you are doing nothing with your life. Everything you do is worthless unless you follow the path. You need to understand that the path was laid before you not because we enjoy telling you what to do but because it is what is meant to be."

Kaylee closed her eyes and pinched the bridge of her nose. This was not the first time she had heard this diatribe from her mother, nor would it be the last. Her mother would likely leave a voicemail and then hand-write a letter to make sure that Kaylee heard it again.

Because this was Angelica Chambers. Nothing was ever good enough. Kaylee had not taken the correct path in life, nor had she followed any path at all in her mother's eyes since she was living like a vagabond, a vagrant. Or so her mother frequently implied.

But Kaylee could stand up for herself. Because while she tried to at least be pleasant in spurts, she also knew when it was time to stop.

"If you're done telling me exactly what to do with my life, I'm going back to work. Yes, as an artist. As a business owner. A successful one, not that you care about any of that. I have earned every single penny I have. Yes, I have the trust, but I haven't touched it. I might because that was the money Grandfather sent for me and saved for me. But I do not have to abide by your rules in order to do so. I married the man you wanted me to marry, and it didn't work out. Let me live my life, Mom."

"You divorced Travis. *Divorced* him."

"Yes, that dirty word called *divorce*. He didn't love me, and I didn't love him. He loved his secretary, or at least he loved doing her on his desk. Which, by the way, is the most cliché thing ever. But it seems that's the thing to do. Because didn't Dad do that, and Grandpa? Or maybe I'm just remembering things that we're not supposed to talk about at the dinner table."

Kaylee hadn't meant to say that last part because she knew it would hurt her mother. But now the words were out there. Her mother was silent for a moment, and Kaylee almost apologized.

Almost.

"You're lucky that I kept you. You're lucky you're still alive to be able to disobey me and act like the ungrateful brat you are. Because while you may have the Chambers last name, and you may have their blood in your veins, you are not a Chambers. I should have gotten rid of you when I had the chance and started over. But, I didn't. Now, you are my cross to bear, and you will do what is expected of you."

Kaylee didn't know what else her mother might say, but she had heard it all before. Instead, she hung up the phone and closed her eyes, trying not to throw up at the idea that her mother had wanted to get rid of her. After all, technically, Kaylee had been a 'seven-month pregnancy.' It was as if she were in Regency Times and, suddenly, she was a perfectly sized, fully matured baby at seven months—also known as: her mother had been pregnant at the time of the wedding.

Angelica had gotten pregnant at nineteen and quietly married Mr. Chambers, Kaylee's father. But now her dad was no longer here, and neither were Kaylee's grandparents. It was just her mother and her, the only family she had left except for the Chambers cousins who fought like cats and dogs.

But she didn't need any of that. She had her life. And she was just fine.

"I have a feeling you just talked to your mother, so, why don't you come over here and into my arms."

She turned on her heels at Landon's words, not having heard him walk in, and threw herself at him. She jumped, wrapping her arms around his neck, and he tightly grabbed her waist. Her tears fell onto his coat, and she was so angry at herself for them.

"I can't believe I let her hurt me this much."

"I only caught the last bit of it, the screaming. I didn't hear the words, but if they're what she said to you in the past, my offer to go and kick her cane out from under her is still available to you."

Kaylee laughed then, her tears drying up even as she felt the ache inside of her.

"I think she'll just come back stronger if you kick her cane out from under her. Maybe add some water, like the wicked witch or something."

"That just might make her stronger, as well. Maybe we should just stay away, just in case."

"How did you know I needed you?" she said after a moment of silence where the two of them just stared at each other, not saying a word.

"I didn't, but I can't stay away from you, Kaylee. And maybe that's the problem."

So, she did what she needed. She kissed him.

CHAPTER 4

*L*andon staggered back, Kaylee's lips on his as he tried to remember his own name. She tasted him, and he tasted her. A little bit of wine, a little mint, and everything Kaylee. He let out a breath, pulling away from her as he cupped her face, his hands digging into her hair.

"Kissing me is not going to solve our problems."

He hated saying the words, but he knew they were important. They couldn't ruin what they had because of base instincts. Or instincts that seemed very useful just then.

"You're the one who kissed me first," she whispered and then laughed. She pulled away, and Landon was colder for it.

"What are we doing, Kaylee?"

"Not fucking, that's for sure." She paused, looked at him like a goddess with paint in her hair and a little bit on her cheek. She had never looked more beautiful, so messy, so…his.

But that was a problem. Kaylee wasn't his.

"I don't know what we're doing," he whispered. "We tried this, didn't we? We both said that this isn't what we needed. We both walked away before we hurt each other."

"And that was over a year ago," she whispered. "Over a year ago, and now we know each other more. And…I don't know. It's just, I think I need to be honest. If I'm not honest, then I'm not myself. And if this ruins everything, then it was meant to be. I just hope our relationship is strong enough for you to understand that I need to say these words. It's just, I can't lie to myself and you and still be me."

He swallowed hard, nodding. That was what he loved most about her. And, yes, he said the word *love*. Fuck it. He loved her. He just didn't know how to say it. She was way stronger than he was at this point if she was willing to say the words. Or say any words at all. Because he had just about swallowed his tongue, and he had no idea what to say next.

"We didn't work out before because I was still hurt from my marriage that didn't end well, and you were on your journey of trying to have the perfect date with every single woman you could." She said the last part wryly, and he chuckled.

"Not quite that."

"No, but you implied that you wanted it to be that way because it made it easier for both of us to walk away. But I'm not where I was then. We've watched every single one of our friends fall for someone, and we tried to help them figure out who they are in order for them to find that path." She paused, giving him a weird look. "*Path*. I can't believe I'm saying the word path."

"What do you mean?" he asked, confused.

"My mother said I wasn't following the right *path*. That it had been laid before me for a reason, and that I wasn't fulfilling my purpose in life."

"Your mother's a bitch."

"Truer words have never been spoken."

"So, don't use the word *path*. If that's the hard word for you."

"All of these words are hard. I wasn't supposed to fall for you, Landon. I wasn't supposed to fall at all. I miss you when you're not around. I miss when you act all protective and caveman-like and then I pretend that I resent it. Because I like it. And you know that I act all cavewoman-like and protective of you at the same time. I miss when you sit in my studio and watch me paint even as you work. I miss when we're not together trying new food. I miss when I'm not ordering with you in mind, knowing that you're going to take half of my food or maybe even more. I miss when we go out as a group, and you and I do our best not to sit next to each other because we don't want others talking about us even though they're totally already talking about us, and we're talking about them at the same time. I miss all of that. And I miss you not by my side. And that should scare me, but it doesn't. And I think *that* scares me even more. So, I'm falling for you Landon. I know I wasn't supposed to. I know we promised each other that we wouldn't do that. But I'm breaking that promise. And I don't know what to say next."

Landon stood there frozen, his hands fisted at his sides as his body shook. It took everything within him not to throw himself at her and make love to her right there on the floor, to prove that she was his just as much as he wanted to be hers.

But he *was* going to do that.

He just needed to say the words first.

"You are so much stronger than I could ever hope to be."

"How can you say that?"

"I can say it pretty easily. I can because you're standing there baring your soul to me when I was trying to figure out exactly what the fuck to say to you. I walked away from you a few nights ago because I didn't mean to kiss you."

She took a step back, her eyes wide, the look in them a little hollow. "Oh. I see. It seems I was mistaken."

He heard the break in her voice, the way she tried to be so strong, and he could have cursed himself.

"No, let me finish." He took two steps forward then, tucking her face between his hands.

"I shouldn't have kissed you because I didn't know if it's what you wanted. I shouldn't have done it because I've been trying *not* to kiss you for far too long. And because as soon as I walked away from you, I knew I was falling for you. But the problem is, I've already fallen. Somewhere along the way, we became each other's other person. I haven't dated a single person since I was with you, Kaylee."

Her eyes widened. "But I thought you had? I…I know you haven't talked about it, but I thought you had."

"No, I haven't. Because every time I thought maybe I could ask someone out, nothing ever came to be. I didn't want it to, I didn't want anyone else. All I can do is think of you. And I wasn't supposed to think of you. We were supposed to just be friends. A year ago, we weren't ready for each other. We had to figure out who we were as ourselves before we could be something more. I know that probably doesn't make any sense."

"I think it makes perfect sense. Why are we so stupid, Landon?"

He lowered his head to hers and closed his eyes. He

inhaled her scent, knowing that this was right. That this had been a long time coming. "We're not stupid. We're just slow."

"Well, that's just mean."

He snorted. "I mean we just took our time figuring out what the next step is."

"And what is the next step, Landon?" In answer, he kissed her again and then lowered her to the floor.

"Landon," she whispered against his lips, and he groaned. "I need you."

He needed her. More than he ever thought possible. So, he kissed her, he bit her chin, and then he leaned over her, remembering their first time and wondering why they hadn't done this again.

Emotions or no.

"I've always needed you, Kaylee. Always."

They were on the floor of her studio, but on the stack of drop cloths she had to the side, the freshly laundered ones with the dried paint. It was as if it had been perfectly made for them.

He kissed her again, letting his lips trail down her jaw and then to the top of her breasts over her tank.

"Make love to me, Landon. Here. In my studio. Where we watch each other and try not to." She rocked against him, and he groaned. He loved when she touched him, when he could feel the heat of her. He'd missed this. Missed this so damn much.

He winked and then took her lips in a searing kiss. "I love watching you work."

"Same. Now, work with me here." They both laughed, and he kissed her again, both of them slowly stripping each other out of their clothes. He loved her body, the way her curves flared and begged for his hands.

So, he touched, her moving down her body as he licked and sucked at her skin. She tasted of peaches, the lotion and scents she used that were so subtle, he could only scent them when he was right on top of her.

Just like he was now.

"Landon," she breathed as he lowered his head to her stomach, gently biting before going lower...then lower. She arched into him again as he tasted her, spreading her for his tongue and fingers.

As he speared her, gently coaxing her closer and closer to the edge, she slid the tips of her fingers over his hair, tugging when he hit that perfect spot.

And when she came, he kept teasing her, his mouth on her clit, wanting one more from her before he came inside her.

"Landon, I can't...I need you inside me."

"One more, Kaylee. I need one more."

"I can't Landon. I can't."

"For me, Kaylee, baby, come for me." And then she did, shouting his name and arching into him once more before he moved away, licking her taste from his lips and moving to hover over her body.

"Inside me. Now." She practically growled the words, and he grinned.

"So impatient. Always wanting more."

She reached between them and gripped the base of his cock, giving it a squeeze and making his eyes cross. "I want *you*, you ass. Now, get this thick thing in me."

"Thick? Aww, baby, you're so sweet."

"If you don't get inside me right now, I'll move and put it in my mouth. Your choice."

He paused, actually thinking about what would be the better option. "Well..." He laughed as she punched his shoulder and then he leaned down, taking her lips again. "Anything you want, Kaylee. Anything."

He didn't want her on the floor, so he flipped them over, and soon, she was straddling him, sliding down his length.

"You're so tight, so perfect for me," he growled.

She tossed her hair over her shoulder and cupped her breasts. "You say the sweetest things."

Then she moved. And he moved. And they moved as one, breathing and rocking into each other.

They had been good before, but now, they were better. Hotter. Needier.

Her hair fell over him in a long curtain of waves and

delicious scent. "Falling for you," he gasped as they moved.

"Always," she whispered, and then they both came, whispering each other's names and aching for one another as if they had been one all along.

And the thing was, they had been. All their dinners, their times together, they'd been just who they needed to be. For themselves and each other.

And maybe, just maybe, they really had been dating all along.

EPILOGUE

*K*aylee ignored the knowing looks at the next game night at Thea Montgomery's house. Oh, yes, all of their friends had known for some time, had actually taken bets on when Kaylee and Landon would finally confess that they were indeed a couple and that, yes, they were in love. Apparently, everyone knew, even though Kaylee and Landon had done their best not to think about it at all.

There was a reason they had not thought about it. They needed time.

Now, they were taking all the time they needed to figure out who they were together.

"Okay, now for the ruler of the bet, I'd like to say thank you, Kaylee and Landon, for deciding to finally reveal your relationship to the rest of us on this date." Adrienne bowed, and the others booed.

"You're serious?" Landon asked as he played with Kaylee's hair. They were sitting on the loveseat, yes, the loveseat because that's where everyone had placed them. He had his arm around her shoulders and was casually coiling her hair around his finger. She wasn't even sure he realized he was doing it.

It was just something that he liked to do because he seemed to love touching her.

He constantly touched her, made her feel alive. She could ignore her mother's desires, ignore the responsibilities she supposedly had.

She could just be.

And she could paint, with whatever medium she wanted. She could just be the Kaylee Chambers she wanted to be, not the one she was apparently *supposed* to be.

"Yes," Adrienne answered, grinning. "Today was the exact date that I picked in the pool, and let me tell you, it's been going on for like four months at this point."

"I cannot believe you beat me by a day," Mace said, wrapping his arms around his fiancée's waist. He smacked a kiss on Adrienne's lips, and the woman laughed.

"Well, it just seems that I'm the best person at this.

The best in the world." Adrienne let out a manic laugh, and everyone giggled as Mace started tickling her.

"I say we play a game of Twister," Dimitri said, his voice low as he gazed at Thea. "You know, since you're already technically playing in front of us." "We will not be playing Twister." Thea raised her chin, trying to look prim and proper.

They all started cracking up because everyone knew exactly what had happened the last time Thea and Dimitri played Twister. Apparently, they had played Twister a few more times since then, sometimes without clothes.

"We will not be playing Twister as a group," Kaylee said, sounding prickly. "We're all close, and very good friends, but Twister turning into a naked group orgy is not something I want to do."

"Oh, thank God," Shea said. "I mean, I already have morning sickness, I don't really need to add anything else vomit-inducing."

"You're serious, right? You're going to be the one who's vomiting?" Shep asked. "These are my sisters and their men. There's no way I want to see any of you guys naked. Well, except for maybe Carter. He's kind of hot."

Roxie choked up a piece of cheese, and Carter pounded her on the back even as he laughed.

Kaylee just shook her head as Ryan and Abby whispered

to each other, a new, pretty ring on Abby's left finger. Nobody had noticed it yet, but Kaylee knew the others would soon. Or maybe they had seen it and were just letting the couple have time to themselves. Everything had moved fast for them, for all of them, and yet not quickly enough at times. They were all growing up and moving on, together.

Before Kaylee opened her shop, before she moved here and found these people, she had thought she would walk alone forever. She had thought that, no matter the steps she took, she would never be enough. But then she found the Montgomerys, found their friends, and found Landon.

And, yes, she knew she was enough.

Maybe she didn't paint by numbers like her mother wanted her to. Instead, she found her own canvas and made her own strokes.

Though, with each step, with each decision and breath she took, she was creating her own masterpiece.

One friendship, one Montgomery, one drop of ink, and one love at a time.

NOW COMES BONUS CONTENT!

The following are bonus scenes and short stories set in the Montgomery Ink world! Each is about a different couple that already have their HEA, so they aren't stand alone romances. In fact, if you haven't read their book, it might be a little confusing.

But I wanted to give a little gift to my readers, so I hope you enjoy it! If you're new to me, these are cute stories that will hopefully make you love my characters as much as I do!

Happy reading!

~Carrie Ann

DELICATE NIGHTS

A MONTGOMERY INK BONUS SCENE

Austin and Sierra from Delicate Ink have weathered terror, angst, and uncertainties but now they're happily married and the parents of two amazing kids. Only problem? They need a night to themselves and a long-awaited Montgomery Ink wedding might just be the perfect way to make that happen.

CHAPTER 1

WEDDINGS

*a*ustin couldn't wait until the reception was over. With so many siblings, it felt as if he'd been in wedding after wedding. And while his family meant everything to him, he really just wanted one night with his wife. Was that so wrong?

Yeah, he loved Alex like crazy and adored the fact that Tabby was now a Montgomery in truth, but he desperately wanted out of his suit.

And if he were honest, he wanted Sierra out of that damn dress of hers even more.

Okay, so maybe not *out* of the dress since now all he could think about was rucking that soft cream and peach lace up her thighs and taking her from behind. He'd tug at her hair, making her arch her back so she pressed her ass back into him as he thrust into her. Her butt would jiggle just right, and he'd have to grip harder, increasing his pace until they both came so hard they fell into a heap of sweaty limbs.

He swallowed hard, thankful that he was sitting down and had the tablecloth to cover his raging erection. Suit pants would do nothing to hide the fact that he was now so damn hard, he was pretty sure he would blow if Sierra so much as brushed against him.

Thankfully, for both of them, she was on the dance floor with their son, Leif, and unaware of where his thoughts had turned. Leif looked over and winked at him, and Austin couldn't help but grin back. Yeah, that kid was a Montgomery through and through.

He still couldn't quite believe that he had a teenager who was almost as tall as Sierra. He'd only had the boy in his life for a few short years, but now that time seemed to be going by faster and faster. Their other son, Colin, was out like a light upstairs in the main house with the four babysitters the family had hired to help ride herd on the Montgomery kids. With so many babies and kids running and crawling around, was it any wonder they'd had to hire out for a Montgomery wedding while they usually tried to take care of their own?

And what a wedding it was. Tabby and Alex had fought hard for their time together, and Austin was damn happy for both of them.

He'd be even happier once things ran down and he could take his family home, get them to sleep, then take his wife to bed.

Yeah, that sounded like the perfect ending to a long day full of family and friends. Even Tabby's family had flown in from Whiskey, Pennsylvania to be with her. Austin always found it weird that she had another family so far away since she was so ingrained in the Montgomerys and had been for so long. But her brothers and parents loved her hard and were pretty kickass people.

But hell, he just wanted everyone to go home so he could. Or at least have things get to the point where no one would notice if he and Sierra walked out after leaving the kids with the grandparents. He was kind of a dick right then for even thinking that, but it had been far too long since he was able to have a night with his wife. He missed her riding his dick as she screamed his name.

They'd been forced to be quiet for far what seemed like ages.

Sierra met his gaze across the dance floor and raised her brow. Yeah, she knew what he wanted, and he knew that she was feeling the same strain he was.

As much as they loved their kids—fucking loved them to the ends of the Earth and back—they needed one night to themselves.

But he had a feeling tonight wouldn't be that night, not with how much fun everyone was having.

Damn weddings.

"Dick straining your zipper, big brother?" Griffin asked as he took the empty seat next to him.

"There a reason you're worrying so much about my dick?"

Griffin snorted and took a sip of his beer. "Not so much. But you keep eye-fucking your wife like you haven't had a taste of her in months." He looked over at Austin. "That about right?"

Austin rubbed his beard with his middle finger. Damn Griffin for being so good at reading people. Made his work as an author better, but damned if it didn't make it hard to keep secrets sometimes.

"Autumn and I can take the kids for you tonight if you want. It might be easier for us to just sleep in your guest room so you don't have to deal with packing up the kids' shit. You and the wife can go get a hotel room and fuck until the sun comes up."

Austin blinked slowly before turning to his brother. "You really think Sierra is going to want to show up with *no* luggage at a hotel? And what about you and Autumn? I'd have thought the two of you would want some time to yourselves. And do I really look that hard-up?" He was a little worried about the answer to the latter since he was in public. No need to appear like some cretin in front of family. He could do that behind closed doors with his wife, thank you very much.

Griffin shrugged. "We have time to ourselves almost every night. Perks of being the best aunt and uncle around, who don't have kids of our own. But I know you and Sierra have been working really hard recently, and with two kids in completely different stages of their lives at home, you probably don't have a lot of time for just the two of you. So let us do this."

Austin frowned, bending forward so his forearms rested on his thighs. "Sierra doesn't like unplanned things."

"She might like this. Autumn can even pack her a bag, and we'll drop it off at whatever hotel you choose later tonight. Go. Have fun, and just be with your wife. We can handle the kids."

Austin ran a hand over his beard and swallowed hard, the idea of having a whole night alone with Sierra far too tempting to pass up. "Let me ask if she had any other plans for us tonight." For all he knew, she just wanted to go home and sleep after a long day of wedding festivities.

Griffin clapped him on the back. "That's what I wanted to hear. Go get your woman."

Austin was already prowling toward the punch bowl

where Sierra stood talking with his sister Miranda. His baby sister must have noticed the glint in his eyes because she quickly skittered away, leaving Sierra snorting over at him.

"Really, Austin? How scary are you trying to be right now?"

"Enough." He quickly went over the plans Griffin had mentioned, and worry briefly crossed her face before she grinned. "What do you say, babe? Wanna take a night with me?"

"You're sure they'll be okay?" She bit into that luscious lip of hers, and he could only imagine how they would look wrapped around his dick.

"The kids, or Autumn and Griffin?" At her look, he ran his knuckles over the bare skin of her shoulder. He loved the way she shivered at just that small touch and couldn't wait to see what else he could do.

"I'd say both but...damn, Austin. I can't get the idea of your dick in my mouth out of my thoughts." She whispered the last part so close to his ear, he could feel the heat of her breath. This, of course, sent his cock straight to the almost-blowing stage, and he had to count to ten backwards before he could even say anything.

"Play with me, Sierra. Just for the night."

"Always."

He was surprised that he refrained from tossing her

over his shoulder and carrying her out of the wedding at her answer, but from the look on his family's faces as they said their goodbyes, he had a feeling it had been close.

Whatever.

CHAPTER 2

BEDSHEETS

"That woman knew I was about to do you right now," Sierra muttered as Austin closed the room door behind them with a loud snick. "I mean, we're wearing *wedding* clothes and just checked in late to a hotel for one night without luggage. That practically screams sexcation."

She turned and watched Austin undo his tie. She was pretty sure if her panties hadn't already been damp from the anticipation of what was to come, she'd have drenched them at the sight. Who knew she could fall in love with wrists and forearms? She'd thought the term *arm porn* was just a joke until she met Austin Montgomery.

"So?" her husband asked. "This is a classy place, and after I fuck you hard a few times, we'll take a bath in that fancy-ass tub, fuck some more, then fuck again in the bed. Or...some mix of that. Then, later, when Griffin shows up with our things, we'll have clothes for tomorrow so we don't have to do the walk of shame. But I don't really give a care that the woman at the front desk knows we're about to have sex. My plan is to make you scream you so loud that she can hear you from there as you come on my cock."

Red Alert.

Wet Panties Ahead.

"Jesus," Sierra muttered. She was one damn lucky woman. And because her thong was far too wet for her to even walk at this point, she did the only thing she could do.

She slid her hands up under her dress and tugged the sides of the lace down before stepping out of them. Austin watched her every movement, the lead pipe behind his zipper growing before her eyes.

She'd always loved that her husband was a grower *and* a shower.

Fucking fantastic.

"Take off the rest of your clothes," she ordered, loving the way he raised his brow at her tone. "I don't want to spend too long trying to get that zipper down, or ending up in half a dress or just one sock. I want us both naked. Now."

"I thought I was the one who gave the orders, babe." His tone was so low, so *demanding*, her knees went weak. It had been so long since they played. They'd grown through the dynamics of their relationship and weren't the same couple they were when they first met. And for that, she was glad.

But right then, she could only strip out of her clothes and go to her knees at his voice, wanting a taste of what they'd once had but knowing it wasn't what they both *needed* any longer.

Just a taste.

Not a forever.

She already had her forever with him. And she loved their present, the promise of their future, but for this moment, they could step into their past and *remember*.

"Damn," he growled low. He stalked to her and ran his thumb over her lips. She opened for him, sucking. "You want my cock in your mouth?"

"Yes, sir." The word felt foreign on her tongue after so long.

He shook his head. "I'm Austin, Sierra. You're mine as I'm yours."

"Then, yes, *Austin*, I want your cock in my mouth."

"Then unzip me and start sucking. I want to come

down your throat while you play with my balls. Then I'm going to eat you out until you run wet down my face. Sound like a plan, babe?"

In answer, she undid his pants and slid him out of his boxer briefs. He was so hard that he was already wet at the tip. She spread the wetness over him, and he shuddered before wrapping her hair around his hand and pulling her head closer to him.

She opened for him, needing him in her mouth. He tasted of salt and man, and she wanted more, *craved* more. Her husband let out a groan, and that just egged her on. So she looked up at him before swallowing him whole.

They both groaned at that, and she closed her eyes, getting to work. She loved going down on him, adored knowing every sound and movement he made was because of *her*.

She'd married the man of her dreams and got to sleep with the man of her heart *and* her fantasies.

She was one lucky Montgomery.

Before she could get her fill, however, Austin was in front of her, his mouth on hers, and his hand between her legs. He moved his hands with the experience of a man who knew his woman as he played with her folds and rubbed her clit.

"I know I said I'd be slow and savor you," her husband growled, "but I can't wait any longer."

In answer, Sierra arched up into him, needing more. "If you don't get inside me right now, I'll scream."

He kissed her harder. "I'll make you scream anyway."

Then she was on her back on the bed as Austin stood at the end of the mattress, thrusting into her with one deep movement. She gasped, his length filling her so completely that she knew she'd be sore in the morning even after all they'd shared together.

And she couldn't freaking *wait*.

They moved together as one, their bodies sweat-slick and aching. She was coming before she could catch her breath, and then she found herself on top of him, riding him until they both came together.

Her nails dug into his skin, and his fingers gripped her flesh to the point of bruising. An aching pain that would be a constant reminder that they'd taken each other to the edge, to the point of ecstasy.

She'd never loved her husband more.

At least, that was what she'd thought until he brought her, breathless, to the tub and leisurely washed her skin, his lips on her shoulder as he achingly cared for her.

No, *now* she'd never loved her husband more.

"Mine," she whispered, her body feeling heavy and sated.

"Always, babe, always."

And then she slept in the arms of the love of her life, knowing that no matter what they went back to the next day, they had this night. And no matter how many years passed, she knew they'd always be breathless for one another, always ache with need at the mere thought of each other.

Sierra Montgomery was one lucky bitch, and she knew it.

Damn straight.

CHAPTER 3

HOME

*A*ustin grunted as Colin stepped on his junk, but since the kid was bouncing on the couch as he wore out some of his never-ending energy, he couldn't really say anything. He hadn't been paying close enough attention and probably deserved a small, sock-clad foot on his crotch.

Sierra met his gaze across the living room as she winked.

He just laughed and set Colin on the floor so he could play with Leif like he had been before he decided to crawl all over his dad.

Austin met his wife's gaze again and couldn't get the image of her naked and sated from the night before out of his mind. They'd made love two more times after their bath and had slept for only a couple of hours before the bellhop had brought up their bags, courtesy of Griffin and Autumn.

And since neither of them could be without their kids for long, they'd had breakfast in bed before coming home and relieving his brother and sister-in-law of their duties. He owed the two of them for sure.

He also knew that Leif was getting old enough to watch Colin on his own. Perhaps, even in a few years. Somehow, his family had grown from just him alone in his house, worrying that he'd never find a way to fill the empty rooms, to something so full, he could barely comprehend it.

It still boggled his mind that he'd once had nothing but his shop and his dreams and now had more than he could ever wish for.

He had two amazing sons—one from a past where he'd lost so much, and the other from his present where he'd almost lost even more.

He had his home and business, a testament to everything he'd gone through.

He had the Montgomerys—those in Denver, Colorado Springs, Boulder, and Fort Collins.

And he had his wife.

His Sierra.

His everything.

What more did a bearded, inked man need?

INSPIRE ME

A MONTGOMERY INK BONUS SCENE

A visit with Shep and Shea from Ink Inspired.

CHAPTER 1

hile numbers usually calmed Shea; today, they only annoyed her. Her head hurt, her back ached, and she hadn't been able to sleep for longer than a few hours at a time since she'd gone back to work. Of course, if she were truly honest with herself, she hadn't slept a full night since before Livvy was born.

Totally worth it, since Livvy was her everything. But right then, all she wanted was a nap.

And a tumble with her husband, Shep.

A long tumble against the door, on the table, or even over the back of the couch. She and Shep weren't much for beds. Or they hadn't been—before Livvy. Now, with a child toddling around and getting into everything with her adorably curious mind, sex outside the bedroom hadn't been on their radar for a bit.

Shea let out a breath and put away her computer. She'd already done her work for the day at the office and needed to get dinner started since Shep would be home any minute. They took turns cooking dinner depending on what shift Shep worked at the tattoo shop. Since she'd gotten home first tonight, it was her turn.

"Mommy!" Livvy tottered her way out of her bedroom and ran smack into Shea's legs.

Letting out a grunt, she bent to pick up her daughter, smothering her baby with kisses. "You want to help Mommy make tacos?"

"Yuck! Cake!" Livvy was at the age where everything *had* to be yelled, even if it didn't make sense. Plus, she only wanted cake. Everything else was *yucky*.

Shea held back a roll of her eyes since Livvy had already caught on to that trait far too early. "Tacos, darling. Not cake."

"Cake!" Livvy yelled once again, a smile on her face.

Shea blew a raspberry on Livvy's cheek, loving the way her baby giggled. "Tacos."

A long sigh. "Okay."

"Thank you for agreeing," Shea said with a laugh and carried her daughter to the kitchen. She set Livvy in her chair and snapped her in place so she wouldn't inadvertently get in the way and hurt herself.

Humming along with the songs that her little girl sang and rambled, Shea browned the meat and stirred the beans while chopping up veggies for the toppings. She was so into what she was doing that she almost screamed when large hands gripped her hips.

Of course, she knew whose hands those were and exactly what the man pressed firmly behind her wanted. She wanted to do the same to him.

"Holy hell, Shep. Don't do that when I'm holding a knife. You scared the crap out of me."

He kissed her neck, the scrape of his beard intoxicating. "I couldn't help it. You were bent over just enough that it put all these dirty thoughts into my head."

She sighed and moved her head to the side as he licked and kissed his way up her neck. "I'm having those dirty thoughts, too."

He bit down, and she shuddered, dropping the knife on the cutting board.

"Da!"

Shea let out a sigh, and Shep gave her a quick kiss over where he'd bitten, then went back to the other woman in his life. She looked over as Shep picked up Livvy, their daughter going into a dramatic recitation of everything that had happened that day as Shep nodded along, a smile on his face.

If she didn't already love him, seeing the big, tattooed man holding the little girl with such rapt joy on his face, would have made her fall for him. As it was, she fell just a little bit more in love with him right then.

"I love you," Shea said with a smile.

Shep turned with Livvy in his arms and grinned. "Yeah? I love you, too."

She licked her lips and went back to browning the meat. "Tacos should be ready soon. Will you set the table?"

"No problem." She heard Shep move around with Livvy in his arms, setting things out on the table and getting her juice cup ready for dinner.

"I thought you'd be later," she said as she served up the meat and toppings.

"Sassy's out for the week on a family vacation, and the others were taking over the shop." He paused. "When you have time tonight, I have something to ask you." At the sound of his serious tone, she looked up.

"What's going on?"

He shook his head as he buckled Livvy back in her highchair. "Let's eat first and get this one ready for bed before we talk."

She sighed. "Well now that you've gotten my interest piqued, I'm worried. What's going on, Shep?"

He kissed her softly. "Good things. At least, I hope."

She pressed her lips together as she pulled away but didn't object when he pulled her onto his lap. She leaned into him, missing his touch more and more these days. His hours had been weird recently at the shop, and he'd been working more than usual. She was starting to get worried.

His body tensed. "Damn, I knew I should have waited to say something," he said after a moment, letting out a breath. "What do you think of Colorado Springs?"

She blinked. "You mean where your sisters and parents live?" She knew everyone used to live in Denver before each set of cousins moved to a different major city in Colorado. She wasn't sure why that had happened, but she figured it had to do with work. Of all of the Montgomery cousins—and there were *a lot* of them—Shep had been the only one to permanently move out of state to New Orleans.

"Yeah. There. Thea, Austin, and Maya have been talking and…well…"

Her eyes widened as he spoke, and she blinked.

Well, that wasn't what she'd been expecting at all. And yet…and yet she knew it was exactly what they needed.

To FIND OUT WHAT HAPPENS NEXT, BE SURE TO READ THE *Montgomery Ink series!*

LONG DAY'S NIGHT

A MONTGOMERY INK BONUS SCENE

Ian's been out of town for far too long but Rafe and Sassy might have a few ideas to…comfort him. Catch their full romance in Ink Reunited.

CHAPTER 1

*T*here was nothing Ian wouldn't do to get back to New Orleans, but he was afraid he'd only see the New York City skyline when he woke for the next few weeks. He might have lived in the city for years before moving back to where he'd grown up, but New York wasn't home anymore.

The acquisition of the new company had taken twice as long as it should have. And because of that, Ian had been stuck in the city with his husband, wife, and twins. It wasn't fair to Sassy or Rafe that they'd been forced to shoulder the burden of daily life with twins and jobs of their own because he'd been stuck up north.

Not only did he hate not seeing them every day other than through Skype, he missed everything about them. He missed the feel of his wife against him as they spooned long into the night just as much as he missed the feel of his husband's strong hands his back after a particularly long day at work. Ian knew he was quite spoiled with the both of them and yet because of his job he hadn't been able to see them and over a month since he'd been in London before this trip as well.

And because of other people's mistakes, it might be another month until he could go back.

That was unacceptable.

It has been a long hard road to go back to New Orleans in the first place I find his happiness in an unlikely pair. Even though the world had set against them, he'd found his happy ever after in not one but two people. They were a true triad. Rafe was as much as his as Sassy was. And the same could be said of the other two. But at the moment, it felt as if he were on the outside looking in.

He hated it.

And yet he knew without asking someone he loved to sacrifice something of theirs, nothing would be changing anytime soon.

Yet sulking around in his penthouse apartment while staring off into the skyline wasn't going to help anyone.

If it wasn't for the fact that he had a planned Skype call with his family, he might have still been in the office, working his butt off, or worse, working in his home office and drinking coffee late into the night. It was no wonder a lot of people in his profession ended up gaining too much weight and had heart attacks because of the stress the fact they didn't eat enough of the good things that kept them healthy.

Ian was afraid too many nights like this and he'd become one of those people.

However the thought of seeing his children's faces tonight, make it all better. Ethan and Lily we're over a year old and now and forming their own personalities apart from each other. Even though scientifically it didn't make any sense, he felt like he saw a little bit of the three of them in his twins. Though they haven't done DNA testing to see who the biological the father was, it was clear that the twins were Rafe's. But Ian felt as if they were his no matter what test results might say. The children knew him as Daddy while Rafe was Papa. He knew it was only going to get harder as the children aged since Ian, Sassy, and Rafe weren't in a conventional relationship, but he knew that he would be there for his children just like his spouses were no matter what.

His phone buzzed reminding him to get on the computer so he wouldn't missed the call and he smiled. Damn he missed them.

As soon as he turned on the screen, the familiar ringing tone started and he answered with a smile. Ray sat across from him now with the twins on each knew.

His husband was beyond handsome and just seeing

him in there made Ian want to groan. Rafe must have caught the familiar glint in his eye because his husband just winked.

He winked back before turning his attention to Ethan and Lily. The other loves of his life. He'd never thought he'd be a father, not after everything that had happened between him, Sassy, and Rafe back when they'd been younger, but now he couldn't even bear to think of his life without the twins.

They were his everything, his future, his peace—even if they kept him up in the wee hours of the night with colic and feedings.

They were *his*.

"Where's Mommy?" Ian asked, disappointed in not seeing Sassy right away.

Rafe shrugged and Ian frowned. "She couldn't make it tonight. Had something to do."

That didn't sound like his wife at all. She might love her job at the tattoo shop and had wonderful friends, but she'd yet to miss a call with him since he'd been gone. He couldn't help but feel that little stab of pain at not seeing her.

What could be so important that she'd miss him?

Of course, that only made him feel like a dick since he was the one out of town, not her.

"Tell her I love her," Ian said, his voice a little hoarse. He swallowed hard before asking the twins about their day. They babbled to him, looking like little miniatures of Rafe and Sassy.

If he'd been unsure at all about his relationship with Rafe and Sassy, the fact that he was so far away and on the outside looking in would hurt him more than he could say. But with these little calls and the letters that Sassy had the twins stamp and color, he felt like he was there, if only for brief moments.

But he still missed his family like hell and wished he didn't have to stay up in the city for so long. He hung up with his family, blowing them kisses so they would giggle and grin, before opening up his calendar.

If he worked at it, he could move a few weekends and get down to New Orleans. He'd be exhausted and use up his miles, but he didn't care. He had money. Hell, he had enough money to buy his own plane.

He just hated not being with his family.

The doorbell rang and he frowned, wondering who the hell could be at his door at this time of the evening on a weeknight. And who would have been able to get up the elevator through security?

Confused, he pocketed his phone and went to answer the door.

When he opened it, his dick hardened and a wide smile crossed his face.

"Sassy," he breathed.

She quirked a brow and put a hand over her trench

coat-clad hip. She'd tasseled her hair and had the highest fuck-me heels he'd ever seen on.

"Hey, Big Boy, I heard you might be lonely and I thought I'd come up to…comfort you."

He growled and tugged on her coat so she slammed into his chest. She laughed and he closed the door behind her, burying his face into her curls so he could inhale her scent.

"What are you doing here?"

"I missed you," she whispered before biting his earlobe. "Rafe will be by next weekend and after that we're bringing up the kids. Then you can try to come down after that. Screw waiting until the job's over. You're ours, Mr. Steele." She cupped him through his pants. "And we don't take no for an answer." She pulled back and winked at him. "Now, darling, why don't you see what I have on under this coat?"

He swallowed hard and tugged on his tie. "Am I going to like it?" he croaked.

"Considering I *forgot* to pack anything at all on this trip? Oh, I think you might."

And when her coat fell to the floor, Ian knew he was one lucky man.

Damn lucky.

NESTING

A GALLAGHER BROTHERS BONUS SCENE

Owen and Liz from Passion Restored are expecting and yet nothing is as expected.

CHAPTER 1

OWEN

"So you want the couch on the other wall?" Owen asked, doing his best not to frown. In fact, if he kept all of his emotions in check and looked as if he truly understood what his wife and the love of his life was saying, he just might survive the final weeks of her pregnancy.

Might being the operative word.

"Yes." Liz nodded, her blond hair swaying around her shoulders. She'd been leaving it down for the past few weeks instead of putting it up in a ponytail, and he liked the look on her. Not that he'd say that because she'd probably find a way to make it sound as if he'd called her a heifer when she had her hair up.

Liz Gallagher, off of work since she'd been forced to

start maternity leave early and almost ready to pop out their baby, was a force to be reckoned with.

Hell, she was a force to be reckoned with on any day. The added stresses just enhanced that.

And, honestly, it made Owen fear for his life and sanity most days.

But he loved her unconditionally. They'd done the whole death-do-they-part thing, and he took his vows seriously.

Hence why he was rearranging their living room for the fourth time since Liz moved in. When they found out they were pregnant, she'd moved into his place from her house next door. His brother and Liz's best friend lived in the other house now, and were on their way to being married and all of that jazz, too, but he honestly couldn't keep his attention on that right now.

Instead, Owen focused on the woman in front of him because if he didn't get this couch in the right position, she might just pull his head from his shoulders with her bare hands. He knew praying mantises were known for eating the heads off their mates, but this was a whole other matter—even if it sort of reminded him of the Discovery Channel scenario.

"If we move the couch, then we'll have to move the TV so you can see the screen."

"And?"

He was one step from walking off the plank.

One with a very, *very* long drop.

"And that means there will be wires across the walkway to the dining room and kitchen. Are you sure you want that?"

"Are you saying I can't make up my mind? That the hormones are making me crazy? Because you're the reason I'm in this mess, Gallagher. Don't fucking test me."

Then she broke down into tears.

So this was being married to the strongest woman he knew when all he wanted to do was hold her close and tell her everything would be okay.

He quickly set down the end of the couch, praying he didn't hurt his back, and ran to his wife. "Baby, what can I do?" He wrapped his arms around her and hugged her close. It was a lot more awkward than it had been when she wasn't carrying their child, but they made it work. His brother, Graham, who had been holding the other end of the couch, thankfully just stood back without saying a word. Since his own wife, Blake, was also pregnant and only a couple of weeks behind Liz, the man understood the precarious situation they were in.

"Make this baby come out because I'm tired and annoyed and making you move things that make no sense. We like order, Owen. Why am I not doing things in order?"

Graham walked past them, lifting his chin in Owen's direction before leaving the house and shutting the front door quietly behind him. Owen would call him back or one of his other brothers if he really needed to move furniture again.

"You're making a person inside you. You're allowed to want things the way you want them."

"And end up with cords in the way so we'll trip and end up in the hospital and not be able to care for the baby? See how I am? Ugh." She tugged on his shirt, letting out a big sigh that went straight to his heart.

"How about we both sit down and talk about this?" He did his best to sound casual, but when she leaned back and rolled her eyes, he knew he hadn't succeeded.

"I love you. Thank you for taking care of me."

He leaned down and touched his lips to hers. "I love you, too. You're everything to me, Liz. You and this baby. So if you want me to move the couch again, I'll call Graham or one of the others to help, and we'll do whatever want. Whatever you need. I promise."

"How about we go back to the bedroom and see how the bed is?" She waggled her brows, and he grinned.

"I like the way you think." He kissed her again, but before he could help her to the bedroom, she leaned back, her eyes going wide.

"Oh, no."

"What?" His heart pulsed in his ears, and he was ready to call an ambulance or the Army if he needed to.

"I think my water broke."

Then he looked down and noticed the wetness on both of their feet as well as their formerly clean area rug.

"Your water broke," he repeated, his voice scratchy. "Holy shit, you're having a baby. My baby. Your baby. *Our* baby."

Then he kissed her again, all thoughts of cords and furniture and his orderly list going right out the window.

CHAPTER 2

LIZ

"**What** do you mean push?" Liz asked, her feet in stirrups, and her body sweaty and aching. "I can't be ready to push. There's no way I'm already dilated and a hundred percent effaced. That's not the order, you guys. I'm a nurse. I need order."

Owen squeezed her hand, and she knew he was thinking the same thing. Order was how they survived, and she knew it wasn't logical for it to remain color-coded and list-oriented once they were parents, but they were going to damn well try.

Her doctor and friend smiled kindly. "You're already there, Liz. The baby is doing great, and so are you. But it's time to push."

"I haven't been in labor long enough," she pleaded.

She'd started off her day going insane moving couches and, apparently, she was just going to keep on that track with the ridiculous things coming out of her mouth.

"The baby wants to come out now," her friend and fellow nurse said softly. "Time to push, Liz."

"I don't have my music."

"Baby," Owen said softly. "Maybe you should just do what the doctors tell you to."

Liz glared at him, and her husband, the love of her life, noticeably paled. "Owen. Gallagher."

He rolled his eyes, then kissed her on the top of the head. He would pay for that later, but first, she had to stop this horrible pain.

"Push, Liz. Let's finish making this baby and meet him. He's as eager as we are."

Tears filled her eyes, and she braced herself for another contraction. "Fine. If everyone else says to."

"Thank you," her husband said and then let out a groan when she squeezed his hand harder.

What? Contractions were a bitch.

She pushed and pushed, screamed, probably really hurt Owen's hand, and pushed some more. And when she heard the first cry, she knew that no matter how many lists she made, she'd never forget this moment, never forget that sound.

She was a mother. Owen was a father.

And another Gallagher was out in the world. Everyone else had better strap in because the Gallaghers were here to stay.

OUTNUMBERED

A GALLAGHER BROTHERS BONUS SCENE

Blake and Graham from Love Restored know once they have their next baby, they'll officially be outnumbered. And they're just fine with that.

CHAPTER 1

BLAKE

*B*lake knew she shouldn't have sat on the floor, but she wanted to rest for a minute, and the laundry was on the couch. So, she'd ended up on a large pillow near the sofa, and figured it might take a crowbar and perhaps a forklift to get up again.

This is what happened when you were almost at your due date and not the spring chicken you once were.

Spring chicken. Hell. She could barely remember how she'd gotten through her first pregnancy with Rowan. It had been over a decade ago, and she'd been alone and scared at the time, and yet she had thought she could face the world.

Then she'd faced it.

Lost.

Faced it again.

And now, she figured she'd finally won.

She was married to a wonderful man. Her bearded and broody construction worker, who knew her inside and out. He might be grumpy, but he was also the sweetest man she knew. In marrying him, she'd gotten his family, too. The Gallaghers were tight-knit and strong. Her two new best friends had married Graham's brothers, solidifying their connections. And since one of Graham's brothers had married into the vast Montgomery family, who also happened to own the tattoo shop Blake worked at, she had an even bigger family.

Coming from a place where she'd thought she would be alone, and then had thought she and Rowan would have to fight alone forever...this meant everything.

Now, she had everything she could ever dream of, including new lives that would be hers and Graham's. Graham had adopted Rowan right after they were married, and now they would have *three* babies.

She had everything.

But she had to pee.

Blake rested her head back on the seat of the couch and resisted the urge to call out for Graham to help her get up. Hell, she would probably need to text him so she didn't have to yell across the house. He was currently in the nursery finishing up the final tweaks since they were about to have two new lives under their roof, along with a tween girl who was driving Blake crazy of late.

How all of that had happened at once, she didn't know, but she was so damn grateful.

And she still needed to pee.

"Graham!" she called out, annoyed because she couldn't lever herself up off the floor. One baby was currently rolling on top of her bladder, and the other was pushing at her lung. There wasn't enough room for her organs and the babies, and her body was just becoming aware of that.

She shouldn't have sat on the damn floor, but pregnancy brain was a cruel mistress.

Her very sweet husband didn't answer since he couldn't hear her over his music, and in her mind, he wasn't so sweet anymore. No, now *she* was the grumpy one.

"Graham!"

No answer.

So she did the one thing that annoyed her about this new tech age but didn't care. If she weren't careful, she'd end up peeing her pants, and that wasn't something she needed to do on her nice carpet.

Blake: *Graham. Come into the living room. I need to pee.*

It didn't take long for him to answer, and because he'd been the best husband ever over the past few months of this pregnancy, he didn't even question why she needed him so she could pee. And he didn't bitch that she was being rude.

Hell, she loved this man and hated part of herself for acting this way.

But she *really* needed to pee.

Graham: *On it.*

He was in front of her in an instant, and only frowned slightly when he noticed her on the floor. But because he was probably afraid of her reaction, he didn't say a word, he just helped her up.

She loved him so damn much.

And when the babies kicked extra hard, she just smiled and leaned into him.

Pregnancy moods were weird and ever in flux, but her family made it all worth it. However, the constant needing to pee? *That* she could do without.

CHAPTER 2

GRAHAM

*G*raham watched his pregnant wife sleeping by his side and couldn't help the grin spreading across his face. If at any point earlier in his life, someone had said he'd become a caveman when his woman was pregnant, he'd have called them crazy.

And yet he was *this* close to beating his chest and growling whenever he watched her walk—or rather, *waddle*—around their house. She was growing two of their kids inside her, and he couldn't wrap his mind around it. Add in the fact that Rowan had read every baby book with them and knew way more about sex and reproduction than a kid her age probably should, and he was just one proud papa.

Apparently, Rowan wanted to be ready for a home

birth in case any of the forty Gallaghers and Montgomerys weren't around to help out.

Blake had kissed their daughter's brow before rolling her eyes. Rowan wanted all the info, but he was pretty sure that Blake also wanted the good drugs.

Since his wife was finally sleeping, he didn't reach out and put his hand on her belly like he normally would have—and wanted to now. He loved feeling his girls kick and reach out. Yeah, he and Blake were having twin girls.

Jesus.

How he was suddenly going to be a father to *three* girls, he didn't know, but he couldn't wait. He'd be outnumbered, four against one, but he'd manage. He was a Gallagher, after all.

His brothers laughed at him and what was to come, but as Owen had a newborn at home, and Jake's wife was currently pregnant with their second child, neither of them could say anything. Knowing Murphy, he and his wife would be joining the brood scene soon, but Graham was grateful that only three of the four wives were pregnant at the moment.

All four, plus the numerous pregnant Montgomery women, would have surely started some kind of ice cream shortage...or maybe the apocalypse.

Blake groaned next to him, and he shot up, instantly worried.

"What is it?" he whispered, knowing she had to be

awake. She didn't sleep well as it was, but she didn't usually groan like that.

"I think…I think my water just broke."

Graham blinked, then grinned when Blake smiled widely, even with the worry, anticipation, and anxiousness in her gaze that had to match his.

It was time.

Finally.

And he couldn't fucking wait.

HIDDEN TRIES

A MONTGOMERY INK BONUS SCENE

Hailey and Sloane from Hidden Ink knew their road to becoming parents would be paved with heartache. Now it's time for the next step.

CHAPTER 1

HAILEY

*T*oday wasn't supposed to be the day that she vomited all over her clothes, but then again, there really wasn't a day for that, was there. Hailey leaned against the cool tile of the wall and willed her body not to betray her. Today was supposed to be momentous. It should have been the day that changed everything.

And thinking along those lines was probably why she needed to throw up in the first place.

"Everything's okay," she whispered to herself, hoping no one would hear. "Everything's going to be okay."

Strong arms wrapped around her waist, bringing her back to a strong chest that simultaneous made her heart race and helped her calm down.

"Breath, Hailey. You're doing good. Just breathe."

Sloane's voice sent shivers down her spine, and she couldn't help but fall in love with him even more.

She rested the back of her head on his chest since, even in her heels, she didn't brush his chin. She loved how big her husband was, how comforting he was to her when some would look at his huge muscles and bald head and might feel intimidated.

Hailey never felt safer than when she was with Sloane.

And considering all the hell she'd been through in her life, having that cornerstone meant everything in the world to her. He'd loved her when she hadn't known she could possibly love herself and had shown her that she was worth more than what she'd given herself credit for.

"Thanks," she whispered. "I was on my way to a panic attack."

He kissed her temple, and she turned in his arms, smiling up at him even as she slowed her breathing. They were standing in the middle of an old building, people milling about them as they waited to hear if their lives were about to change.

And what made it all slam into her over and over again was that even after today when her world might forever be changed, it could still shift again and again and again.

"It's going to be okay, baby. You need to have faith."

She looked up at her husband, amazed at his words and the fact that she knew he believed them. Because this was the same man who had looked into the darkness and came back shadowed. He'd fought the fire and had not only been burned, but he could *still* feel the heat on nights when the memories were too much.

But he believed in what they were doing.

Because she did, as well.

"I do. And you being here with me tells me that we're doing the right thing."

He kissed her then, not too hard, but just enough to remind her of one more reason she loved him.

"Of course, we are. Those kids need us, baby. And I can't wait to be a fucking dad."

He'd whispered the last part, aware that others were looking at them.

It hadn't been easy to get to this part of the adoption process, but here they were. Thanks to her treatments for breast cancer as well as injuries Sloane had sustained over in the desert, they'd both known that having a biological child wouldn't be an easy option. And in the end, they'd decided to help a child who needed them, one who was already in this world.

They'd known Grace for a while now, had worked through the foster-to-adopt program to start the process of making Grace theirs in truth. Grace, at age four, was Hailey's daughter now, even though the paperwork wouldn't be complete for another hour or so.

Complete.

As in, Grace would be *theirs*.

And she was so damn worried that it was all going to slip through her fingers in the next hour if, somehow, they found more of Grace's family. Only Hailey knew that would be difficult, as Grace's mother had died three months ago delivering Grace's brother, Oliver.

Hailey sucked in a deep breath, trying not to think about the horridness and how scared the young woman had been when everything changed for her. Both Grace and Oliver had been born with drugs in their system, and Hailey and Sloane both knew that there would probably be issues they would have to deal with as a family.

But they would be a family.

"We're going to have two babies soon, Hailey. Two children who need us, who need love, and who we can be the best parents in the world to. The paperwork is almost done. We've been waiting years for this. We can do this, Hailey. We've got this."

And before she could say anything, the doors opened, and Grace ran through toward them. Sloane went to his knees, holding his arms out for the little girl.

Grace it seemed, was a Daddy's girl.

And Hailey would not let the tears fall as Grace wrapped her arms around Sloane's neck for a hug, babbling about her day.

Hailey ran her hand over the little girl's hair, but her

attention was on the two social workers walking through the door, one with a little bundle in her arms.

Hailey would eventually think about all the legal work that would come after this, and everything that might come later. She knew the details, knew that there would be calls to the house later, name changes, long talks with both children about who their birth parents were.

There would be time for everything.

Because there *would* be time.

But right then, she could only look down at the little boy the social worker put in her arms. Little Ollie, who smiled up at her. Sure, it might be gas, but he was *hers*.

At least, he would be.

Sloane wrapped his arm around her shoulders, Grace leaning down from her spot on his hip to look at her little brother. And Hailey couldn't help the tears that came.

This was her family, her future.

Her son, daughter, and husband.

Sure, the details and legal things would be there later. The paperwork would come. The long nights of worry and not knowing what to do were on the horizon.

But in her mind, this was the anniversary of when they became a family.

Of when their lives had changed.

This was their new life.

Hidden ties and all.

THAT WHISKEY NIGHT

A WHISKEY AND LIES BONUS SCENE

What happened between Fox and Melody before the start of Whiskey Reveals?

1. Whiskey.
2. Some flirting.
3. More whiskey.
4. And…

CHAPTER 1

ox needed a drink. Or four. Thankfully his brother not only ran a whiskey bar, but said bar was in walking distance of his house. He could easily drink until his head stopped hurting before making his way home. Of course in the morning his head would hurt for a whole new reason, but it would be worth it.

He'd had issue after issue crop up at work and if he wasn't careful he'd end up throwing his laptop through the window, screaming as it fell from his second floor office as it smashed onto the sidewalk below. Two of his staffers were in a pissing contest about a lead and another was itching for more space on the front page. He was behind on his own story for next week because he'd been putting out fires thanks to other people. Then someone had switched out the wrong photo below the fold on the front page and he'd had to deal with the ramifications of that for most of the day.

He wasn't adverse to his writers pushing each other to write better and get better stories out there, but the way they were going about it at the moment was going to make him hit something.

And since he only hit his brothers when they were rough housing around, that meant he'd have to hit himself or some other odd crap that made no sense.

"Jesus." He seriously needed that whiskey or he'd end up talking in circles about insane things that only sent him further over the edge. He ran a hand through his hair, then jogged across the street, jaywalking like an idiot rather than making his way to a cross walk. He knew he needed to set a better example for the tourists in town, *but* he really needed that drink and just hoped his mom didn't see him.

Thirty-two years old and he was afraid of his mother's wrath when it came to him breaking the rules.

Sounded about right for his family.

He waved at a few store owners as he passed, smiling though his headache hadn't abated. It was just about dinner time, so the rush of late shoppers before the stores closed was in full swing. He'd been later than he'd liked getting out of his office, so he just hoped that there would be a place for him at the bar. If not, he'd go to the normal booth his family liked to take if it was open. He was easy as long as he could get his whiskey that night.

Dare was working behind the bar when he got in and the place was pretty packed. Kenzie, Ainsley and a couple others were in the family booth. He waved at them, but took one of two empty seats at the bar instead of joining. He'd go over and say hello, be sociable, after he at least had a glass of whiskey in his system.

He started off with a soda and lime and a glass of water, just to make sure he didn't end up with too much of a hangover. Then Dare poured him two fingers of his favorite Whiskey and he saluted, grateful his brother knew him so well.

He downed the soda, then sipped at his whiskey while keeping his water at hand for after the first glass.

That's when he saw her.

All curves and blonde hair. She had a smoky glance that matched the whiskey on his tongue. She wore a black dress that hugged her hips, full breasts, and wore ballet flats that didn't look out of place with the rest of her outfit.

Her gaze traveled over the room before landing on the stool next to him. Fox's dick stiffened ever so slightly under the zipper of his jeans, filling out even more as she sashayed her way across the room and to his side.

"Mind if I take a seat?"

Her voice was smooth, a little low, and went straight to his cock.

"It's all yours." He turned on his stool to get a better look at her. "I'm Fox."

She smiled at him, coy and sexy as hell. "Melody. What are you drinking?"

"Macallan. The good stuff but not the scary good stuff as I need a savings account." He winked and she gave him a grin. "Want a taste?"

Her gaze went straight to his mouth, her tongue darting out to lick her lips. "I'll order my own, Fox. But it does sound good. What better drink to have than whiskey while in Whiskey?"

Dare filled Fox's glass again after pouring Melody two fingers. His brother walked away as the two of them clinked glasses, their gazes on each other, the heat between them intensifying as they sipped.

After her first drink, he pointed out his family members and the fact that Dare owned the bar.

After the second, she leaned closer, her smile sultry as she made him laugh with a joke.

After the third, his dick was so hard he was ready to burst, paying no heed to the idea of whiskey dick.

After the fourth, he paid the bill, and led Melody out of the bar, her side pressed to his. They both beyond buzzed, but not drunk. He was going to take her home, get more water in her, and be sure what was promising between them was what she wanted. He might be pretty far gone himself, but he wasn't going to take advantage.

As Ainsley had told him one, consent was sexy.

"Want a glass of water?" he asked, his hand trailing down her hip once the two of them were inside his place.

"We had a glass of water with each pour of whiskey. We both know what this is. Do you want me to say it? Want me to make it clear?"

He pressed her into the door, her breasts soft against his chest she rocked into his cock. "Say it, Melody. Tell me what you want."

"I want you to fuck me. Hard. Easy. However we both decide. But it's my choice just as much as yours. One night. No promises. Fuck me, Fox."

He kissed her hard as soon as she said his name and she moaned into him. He had his hands on her ass, molding her sweet flesh with his fingers before lifting her up. She wrapped her legs around his waist, pressing her soft heat along the rigid line of his erection.

He sucked on her neck, biting down gently. She tugged on his shirt, gasping into him as he rotating his hips ever so slightly. When he reached between them, sliding his fingers over the cotton of her panties below her dress.

Drenched.

"So wet for me already." He licked her earlobe before biting down on the flesh.

"Fox. Make me come already."

He bit her lip, grinning after he licked the sting. "So greedy." Then he wrapped his fingers around her panties, tugged them to the side, then slide a finger inside her. "So hot." He pumped once. Twice. "So ready."

"Fox," she panted.

He fucked her with his fingers, curling them to find that perfect spot, and when she shattered on his hand, he held her close, taking each ounce of her orgasm for himself.

Then he took her upstairs, stripped her out of her panties, tossing them to the floor, and went to his knees above her. He stuck his head under her dress and his mouth on her pussy, his tongue diving deep.

"Such talent," she panted, her hand in his hair.

He hummed along her clit, sucking and licking. She came again quick and as she was still shaking, he stood up and stripped of his clothes. She was taking off her dress and bra in the next moment, both of them too turned on to bother with the slow seduction.

They'd already been seduced over the smoke and temptation of whiskey.

This was the only logical step.

He had her on her back, a condom rolled over his length, and was inside her in one thrust. He sucked on her nipples, biting hard, as she racked her fingernails down his back. He knew he'd have marks the next day and he was glad. She'd have his marks on her neck and inner thighs, a reminder of what they'd done.

And when she met his gaze and squeezed her inner walls, he was lost. He moved with abandon, his body pounding into hers as she met him thrust for thrust.

He went to his back, letting her ride him, then pulled out and put her on her stomach so he could fuck her hard into the mattress. Then somehow, as the whiskey pushed them harder, she was on her back again and he was on top of her.

He came again with her, and then tried to catch his breath as they both lay sweat slick and panting.

Round two went slower than the first, her mouth on his dick one of the most blissful moments of his life.

Round three was just as fast as the first, her face against the wall as he fucked her, the mirror to the side giving them a show.

Before they could try for round four, they fell asleep, passed out and spent.

And when Fox woke up, he was alone in a cold bed, but not surprised.

Her panties lay on the floor and a note was the pillow next to him.

Fox let out a breath, rolling to his back as his head spun, but he knew his world had been rocked not from the whiskey, but from the woman he could still smell on his skin and in his sheets.

He'd just had the best one-night-stand of his life and now she was out of his life, probably forever.

A smile spread over his face, remembering her when she came on top of him that last time. She'd been fucking perfect. And yet he wouldn't see her again. That twinge of something he rather not name echoing slightly louder.

Melody was gone, but he knew he'd always remember her and their whiskey night.

Not a bad way be remembered.

Not one bit.

A NOTE FROM CARRIE ANN RYAN

Thank you so much for reading **The Bonus Ink Set.** I do hope if you liked this story, that you would please leave a review! Reviews help authors *and* readers.

Executive Ink, Second Chance Ink, and Ink By Numbers were full romances about fan favorite characters who I knew needed an HEA, but not a full book since their romance was cemented earlier in the series. I'm so glad I was able to write their HEAs and give them what they needed!

I hope you enjoyed the other bonus scenes in the set! These were fun stories I wrote for my newsletter in the past. Make sure you're signed up for any more in the future!

Don't miss out on the Montgomery Ink World!

- Montgomery Ink (The Denver Montgomerys)
- Montgomery Ink: Colorado Springs (The Colorado Springs Montgomery Cousins)
- Montgomery Ink: Boulder (The Boulder Montgomery Cousins)
- Gallagher Brothers (Jake's Brothers from Ink Enduring)
- Whiskey and Lies (Tabby's Brothers from Ink Exposed)
- Fractured Connections (Mace's sisters from Fallen Ink)
- Less Than (Dimitri's siblings from Restless Ink)

If you want to make sure you know what's coming next from me, you can sign up for my newsletter at www.CarrieAnnRyan.com; follow me on twitter at @CarrieAnnRyan, or like my Facebook page. I also have a Facebook Fan Club where we have trivia, chats, and other goodies. You guys are the reason I get to do what I do and I thank you.

Make sure you're signed up for my MAILING LIST so you can know when the next releases are available as well as find giveaways and FREE READS.

Happy Reading!

Want to keep up to date with the next Carrie Ann Ryan Release? Receive Text Alerts easily!

Text CARRIE to 24587

ABOUT THE AUTHOR

Carrie Ann Ryan is the New York Times and USA Today bestselling author of contemporary, paranormal, and young adult romance. Her works include the Montgomery Ink, Redwood Pack, Fractured Connections, and Elements of Five series, which have sold over 3.0 million books worldwide. She started writing while in graduate school for her advanced degree in chemistry and hasn't stopped since. Carrie Ann has written over seventy-five novels and novellas with more in the works. When she's not losing herself in her emotional and action-packed worlds, she's reading as much as she can while wrangling her clowder of cats who have more followers than she does.

www.CarrieAnnRyan.com

MORE FROM CARRIE ANN RYAN

Montgomery Ink: Colorado Springs
Book 1: Fallen Ink
Book 2: Restless Ink
Book 2.5: Ashes to Ink
Book 3: Jagged Ink
Book 3.5: Ink by Numbers

The Fractured Connections Series:
A Montgomery Ink Spin Off Series
Book 1: Breaking Without You
Book 2: Shouldn't Have You
Book 3: Falling With You
Book 4: Taken With You

The Montgomery Ink: Boulder Series:
   Book 1: Wrapped in Ink
   Book 2: Sated in Ink
   Book 3: Embraced in Ink

The Less Than Series:
   A Montgomery Ink Spin Off Series
   Book 1: Breathless With Her
   Book 2: Reckless With You
   Book 3: Shameless With Him

The Elements of Five Series:
   Book 1: From Breath and Ruin
   Book 2: From Flame and Ash

Montgomery Ink:
   Book 0.5: Ink Inspired
   Book 0.6: Ink Reunited
   Book 1: Delicate Ink
   Book 1.5: Forever Ink
   Book 2: Tempting Boundaries
   Book 3: Harder than Words
   Book 4: Written in Ink
   Book 4.5: Hidden Ink
   Book 5: Ink Enduring
   Book 6: Ink Exposed

Book 6.5: Adoring Ink
Book 6.6: Love, Honor, & Ink
Book 7: Inked Expressions
Book 7.3: Dropout
Book 7.5: Executive Ink
Book 8: Inked Memories
Book 8.5: Inked Nights
Book 8.7: Second Chance Ink

The Gallagher Brothers Series:
A Montgomery Ink Spin Off Series
Book 1: Love Restored
Book 2: Passion Restored
Book 3: Hope Restored

The Whiskey and Lies Series:
A Montgomery Ink Spin Off Series
Book 1: Whiskey Secrets
Book 2: Whiskey Reveals
Book 3: Whiskey Undone

The Talon Pack:
Book 1: Tattered Loyalties
Book 2: An Alpha's Choice
Book 3: Mated in Mist
Book 4: Wolf Betrayed

Book 5: Fractured Silence
Book 6: Destiny Disgraced
Book 7: Eternal Mourning
Book 8: Strength Enduring
Book 9: Forever Broken

Redwood Pack Series:

Book 1: An Alpha's Path
Book 2: A Taste for a Mate
Book 3: Trinity Bound
Redwood Pack Box Set (Contains Books 1-3)
Book 3.5: A Night Away
Book 4: Enforcer's Redemption
Book 4.5: Blurred Expectations
Book 4.7: Forgiveness
Book 5: Shattered Emotions
Book 6: Hidden Destiny
Book 6.5: A Beta's Haven
Book 7: Fighting Fate
Book 7.5: Loving the Omega
Book 7.7: The Hunted Heart
Book 8: Wicked Wolf
The Complete Redwood Pack Box Set (Contains Books 1-7.7)

The Branded Pack Series:
(Written with Alexandra Ivy)

Book 1: Stolen and Forgiven

Book 2: Abandoned and Unseen

Book 3: Buried and Shadowed

Dante's Circle Series:

Book 1: Dust of My Wings

Book 2: Her Warriors' Three Wishes

Book 3: An Unlucky Moon

The Dante's Circle Box Set (Contains Books 1-3)

Book 3.5: His Choice

Book 4: Tangled Innocence

Book 5: Fierce Enchantment

Book 6: An Immortal's Song

Book 7: Prowled Darkness

The Complete Dante's Circle Series (Contains Books 1-7)

Holiday, Montana Series:

Book 1: Charmed Spirits

Book 2: Santa's Executive

Book 3: Finding Abigail

The Holiday, Montana Box Set (Contains Books 1-3)

Book 4: Her Lucky Love

Book 5: Dreams of Ivory

The Complete Holiday, Montana Box Set (Contains Books 1-5)

The Happy Ever After Series:

Single Title: